MABEL
AND
EVERYTHING
AFTER

About the Author

Hannah Safren graduated in 2012 from Shepherd University where she competed on the women's basketball team while obtaining a degree in sport communication and marketing. In 2013, she published her first book, *Dive*, under Write Bloody Publishing before jumping into architectural sales at Polyglass, USA. She resides in Wilmington, NC with her wife and their two kids, June and Jett. The Safren crew spends their time enjoying the outdoors, drinking strong coffee, and sipping neat bourbon.

MABEL
AND
EVERYTHING
AFTER

HANNAH
SAFREN

BELLA
BOOKS

2022

Bella Books, Inc.
P.O. Box 10543
Tallahassee, FL 32302

Printed in the United States of America on acid-free paper.

First Edition - 2022

Editor: Heather Flournoy
Cover Designer: Sheri Halal

ISBN: 978-1-64247-390-2

Acknowledgments

Big thank you to Rachel Safren, Brittany Deal, Brooke Henderson, Nikki Kuhn, Caitlin Rosing, Jules Stewart, and Claire Winik for your time. The most valuable gift one can give.

Dedications

Mabel and Everything After is dedicated to my wife, Meagan, whom I begged to date me after our summer fling but made me wait for four long years.

2008

MAY

Tuesday, May 27

Massive screens flood Washington Boulevard and every penny-pinching twenty-something is sipping two-dollar Bohs.

"Lou!" I shout over the masses, pointing to the heavy rain clouds overhead. "Let's head in!"

A flood of tipsy onlookers take the cue and maneuver their way into Pickle's Pub: a neon-green Baltimore staple, just across the street from Camden Yards Stadium.

Lou, short for Louanne, is already lining up tequila shots with the bartender's eager assistance by the time I shove my way over to her. "Louie, really?" I nudge. "I thought you were driving us home tonight?"

Home is Shepherdstown, West Virginia. A solid hour, plus, from Baltimore.

"Relax, Emmy!" Lou nods toward the bartender. "My good friend, Pete, here has bought us a round."

She has definitely never met Bartender Pete before, and the way that she is avoiding eye contact tells me that she knows I know that.

Lou and I play on the Shepherd University women's basketball team. We are both majoring in Recreation and Leisure Studies, and we share an apartment. This simply means that we spend entirely too much of our time together.

"Emma, meet my friends." Lou steps back from the bar, flinging her perfect auburn hair over her shoulder. "This is Mabel and her boyfriend, Jack."

I instantly recognize Mabel's name. Lou and Mabel had worked together at River Rat's Rafting as river guides last summer. Just recently, Lou shared how bummed she was that Mabel, her "favorite work friend," wasn't coming back for a second season.

I offer Mabel and Jack a polite smile before redirecting my concerned glare toward Lou. A glare that Lou, once again, hastily diverts by passing the tequila shots around.

"Mabel and Jack, this is my high-strung roommate, Emma." Lou puckers up and gulps down the tequila. No salt, no lime. I follow suit, as do Mabel and Jack.

The sting of the liquor hardly settles before Lou turns to whisper, "We'll stay at my friend Matty's tonight. He lives just down the street, in Fed."

The mile walk from the stadium to the Federal Hill neighborhood isn't my concern. My concern is that I've been friends with Lou for three years and have never, ever heard of this "Matty" guy before.

"Won't Max wonder where you are?" I quiz.

Max and Lou have been dating for about eight months. It's still early, but it feels seasoned. She loves him, glows when he's around her.

"Matty is his friend! Max is the one that suggested we stay with him."

I roll my eyes in annoyance with the predictable situation.

"It's right down the street, Em. Please," she begs.

Realizing I'm not going to consent willingly, she hurries off to another rowdy group of orange and black. Jack disappears in the same breath, stumbling toward the bathroom, leaving Mabel and I to force a friendship at the bar.

"You're not surprised, are you?" Mabel asks, referring to my apparent disappointment in Lou.

"Not the slightest," I mutter, waving Bartender Pete back over. Clearly, during Mabel's one summer working with Lou, she picked up on the three most important factors to consider when venturing out on a drinking escapade with Louie:

1. She is the queen of all social bees.
2. She cannot say no to a good time.
3. She is an incredibly unreliable designated driver.

"What are you drinking, Mabel?"

"Natty Boh."

"Two of those please."

Bartender Pete slides two icy cans down the chipped wooden bar, and Mabel and I *cheers* before swigging back the first gulp.

"I've heard a lot about you, Emma."

The pureness in Mabel's voice shifts my entire body toward her.

"Lou's a big fan of yours," Mabel continues.

Her long, thick maple hair is braided loosely over her right shoulder. She has a faded orange bandana tied lightly around her neck, which highlights her piercing seaweed eyes and emphasizes the dark freckles painted across her cheeks and her nose, and even the lobes of her ears. She is quite the beauty.

"Lou's obsession with me is a bit odd, huh?" I grin, hoping my witty response will overshadow my delayed response. I take a large gulp before changing subjects. "Where do you live, Mabel?"

"With my parents, in Frederick—just for the summer. I go to school down in Wilmington, North Carolina, at UNCW."

I know Frederick fairly well. It's not too far from Shepherdstown, forty-five minutes at most, just over the Maryland border. I'm not as familiar with Wilmington, but I know enough about its neighboring coastal cities to keep the conversation flowing.

"Wilmington is a cool place," I tell her. "I've been a few times for lunch. Right there along the waterfront."

"Yes." Her face lights up. "I love that part of town. So many great restaurants. What brought you there?"

"My grandparents lived in Southport for years," I tell her. "So we'd make our way to Wilmington every now and then to switch it up."

Southport is a quaint coastal town about thirty-five minutes south of Wilmington. Red brick sidewalks. Live oak trees dripping in Spanish moss. Every porch dressed in red, white, and blue. It's a popular filming destination for television and movies, but outside of Hollywood, its charm attracts retirees and red-nosed, rubber-boot fisherman.

"No way!" Mabel's face ignites again. "I love that little town. When my brother comes down to visit, we go fishing off the Southport Fishing Pier." Her smile is warm, her lips lush and captivating. "I'm actually contemplating moving there next summer after school ends."

"To prolong the inevitable?" I chuckle.

"Basically. My friends own a fish shack on the Intracoastal there, so I figure I can work a little and fish a little and read a dumb romance novel or two while I figure out the next move."

"Ah, cheesy romance novels. My favorite."

She winks. "Who doesn't enjoy a good love story?"

* * *

The Orioles beat the Yankees ten to nine in extra innings. My boozy victory toast with Mabel is interrupted by Jack, whom I forgot even existed.

"Let's go, babe," he slurs, flinging his chiseled arm around Mabel's neck. Her petite but sturdy frame is accentuated next to Jack's bulky build. His pigeon-toed posture and heavy, bloodshot eyes confirm that it is, indeed, time for him to leave.

"Okay then," Mabel agrees in good spirit. She wraps one arm around Jack's waist to help balance him, and with her free hand, she gently brushes my arm, grazing my fingertips before pulling away. Her touch sends an unexpected shiver up my spine. We lock eyes, just a breath longer. Does she feel what I feel? I shake the thought with a blink and a smile. "It was so nice finally meeting you, Emma." And off she goes, arm in arm with her staggering partner.

* * *

It's nearly two in the morning by the time Lou and I fall victim to mysterious Matty's hand-me-down jean couch, a likely stolen-slash-prized possession from his fraternity years.

"How many people do you think have had sex on this couch, Emma?" Lou wonders aloud.

"We'll wake up itching and you're to blame."

"Yes," Lou admits. "I am to blame."

I actually don't mind the couch much at all; I'm too preoccupied with thoughts of Mabel. There is something about her effortless charm that's possessing my tipsy thoughts. Is she thinking about me too?

"How long has Mabel been with Jack?" I ask.

"Couple of years, I think," Lou mumbles, nearly asleep. "Max doesn't think she loves him. I think she's been dragging it out a little long as well. I also think Jack's kind of a dick. A varsity one-upper."

"Really?" I ask, not expecting such a harsh response from Lou.

"Who knows, maybe they're meant to be, and we'll have to pretend I never said any of this," Lou drones with her eyes closed. "I just hope they're not."

I smile at her drunken declaration, secretly hoping for the same, before dozing off beside her.

Journal: Wednesday, May 28, 2008

I've met a girl with seaweed eyes. She's swimming through me.

JUNE

Sunday, June 1

"What time do you get off work?" Lou says on the phone.

"I'm done," I huff, speed walking. "On my way home now. I'm basically ready, though."

"Of course, you are." *Click.*

Mine and Lou's two-bedroom apartment is on the east end of downtown Shepherdstown, walking distance to Betty's Diner, an old Civil War hospital turned bar, and my new summer job at the Sweet Shoppe.

It's only been a few weeks, but I'm loving the new gig. The West German Street bakery is known for its decadent chocolates, freshly baked breads, and most notably, its paranormal presence. I haven't yet experienced any fantastical being, but I sure enjoy sharing the hand-me-down tales with the patrons and, of course, drinking way too much breakfast blend.

"Let's go!" I excitedly shove open the creaky front door to our apartment.

When Lou and I moved in last May, we scrubbed the thin-planked wood floors and dressed up the off-white (probably lead) painted walls with yellow string-light bulbs. We lit lemon soy candles and stocked our kitchen with farmers' market greens and the cheapest of beers. By our third afternoon nap on our Craigslist couch, we felt right at home. Sure, the doors could use a little WD-40, but the whole building, much like our lives, is a constant work in progress.

I hustle back to my bathroom, run a brush through my shoulder-length dark hair, slip on a clean V-neck T-shirt, and tuck it into the same high-waisted jeans I wore to work today. And yesterday.

"I love the look, Emma," Lou sarcastically digs, as she so often does about my style.

My "look" for Cool Night is exactly as it is for work, and for school, and for most other occasions. I like to think I'm simple and stylish, but Lou has coined my attire as "Lesbianish."

Lou's clothing preference doesn't vary much from mine. The difference, of course, is that she's a bit spunkier, often spinning thick windy curls into her lush auburn hair, and God forbid she leaves the house without poppy-red lipstick or some subtle glossy finish.

"Well, you'd be a six-pack in already if you hadn't spent the last hour primping for a *bonfire*."

Lou chuckles. "We can't all be breathtaking lesbians like you. I'll be ready in five."

The newly organized Sunday evening bonfire had only begun three weeks earlier, at the end of the school year. Max had come over to kick off the summer with Lou and me. Somehow, two Natty Bohs and a tree-hugger conversation about hiking the C&O Canal inspired us to build a bonfire. We stole a shovel and a pile of mossy stones from a remote graveyard on the outskirts of town. Within the hour we were lighting up a teepee of logs, texting everyone we knew to come join us, and deeming Sunday night, for the rest of the summer, Cool Night.

Lou takes the credit for officially titling the Sunday evening event. On the night we built that first bonfire, Lou was wearing a backward camo baseball cap, which she claimed made her look cool, hence, Cool Night.

Brilliant.

Shepherdstown needed a Cool Night. The town yawns through the summer. It's home to roughly forty-five hundred students when classes are in session, but when the university closes, the population tails off to less than half of that. It's mostly boutique shop owners, the River Rats (Lou and all her buddies that work as rafting guides on the Potomac River), aged professors, and, of course, a few athletes like me and Lou that stick around to utilize the campus amenities.

I personally think the quaint town is best when boring. It doesn't hurt that our rent drops to a summer special of four hundred dollars per person a month, and with another thirty a week we can eat and drink our way through every happy hour in town.

"I can't believe the cops haven't shut this down yet," Lou says as we stroll up to the abandoned parking lot. There is already a group of River Rats stacking up the wood logs. "I mean, aren't we loitering, or breaking and entering, or too noisy?"

I can't believe it either. It seems every party we attend during the school year gets shut down sometime between midnight and two a.m. I suppose there isn't much else for cops to do in a small college town. Other than address the frequent paranormal claims.

"Maybe the cops are taking the summer off," I say. "Or maybe they know we've constructed this pit with stolen graveyard goods, so they're leaving the cuffs to karma."

"The latter," Lou confirms. "Definitely the latter."

* * *

The evening is teetering right around eighty degrees. Not a cloud in the entire West Virginia sky. Max set up his speakers, and he and Lou are playing a competitive game of one-on-one cornhole to Pandora's Top Country playlist.

"Hey, Emma."

I look over my shoulder and butterflies instantly erupt within me. "I didn't know you were coming, Mabel! Jack here too?" I feel my face redden, flustered by her presence. Hoping I didn't sound too overly elated to see her.

"Not tonight." She shrugs off the question, bracing for Lou's attack.

"So happy you're here!" Lou exclaims, slamming into Mabel and squeezing her much too tightly. "She's staying with us tonight, Emma. Drink up, ladies!"

We all *cheers*, but before I can muster up a conversation with Mabel, Lou drags her into a circle of River Rats. Mabel and her old work buddies spend the entire evening hysterical over stories from their Harpers Ferry summer. And I spend the entire evening wishing Mabel would excuse herself from the group long enough for me to approach her.

* * *

"Can I join you?" Mabel asks, already sliding into the neighboring folding chair. Much of the crowd dispersed with the midnight hour.

Finally. I smile warmly, welcoming her company. "So, what do you think of Cool Night?"

"So cool," she says, giggling. "I haven't seen a lot of those guys since last summer. It was fun catching up with them. How about you? Are you having fun?"

Her face is soft against the fire's light, her gaze sturdy on mine. She doesn't flinch, doesn't even blink when we make eye contact. There is an intimacy in her stare that I'm not certain I'm misconstruing.

"Where is Jack?" I probe, disregarding her follow-up question.

Mabel shifts her eyes from me to the fire and reaches for her nearly empty bottle of Bud Light Lime. "We aren't together."

Instinctively, I reply, "I'm so sorry."

Lou conveniently interjects into the odd moment. "I'm gonna go back to Max's tonight. Mabel, you can have my room."

"Thanks, Louie." Mabel nods.

"You girls can handle putting out the fire?"

"We got it," I assure Lou.

The crackling wood and whispers from the towering trees overhead play softly as Lou and Max, hand in hand, dash farther and farther down the street.

It's just Mabel and me now.

"Are you seeing anyone, Emma?" Mabel asks.

I think of my extended fling with Alli, whom I'd met at a free yoga class in the fall at Morgan Grove Park, but Alli only calls me when she is drunk, and I only respond to Alli when I'm drinking. Lou thinks Alli is a user. I think Alli is just lonely, and sometimes I'm lonely too.

"No."

Hour after hour, Mabel and I carry on about thrift store finds, favorite grocery stores, our go-to nail polish colors, how we'd like to hike Machu Picchu. All while tossing empty beer bottle after empty beer bottle into the pop-up green trash can beside the firepit.

I peek down at my watch, squinting to make out the numbers in the darkness. "My gosh, Mabel, it's nearly five a.m." Though the last embers are hardly breathing, I pour the rest of my water bottle over the pit for good measure.

"I can't remember the last time I pulled an all-nighter," she ponders aloud.

"I'm not sure I ever have." I laugh, reaching for her hand to lift her from her chair. She reaches back instantly, tightly securing her hand in mine, and once again I don't expect my body to react, but it warms on contact.

"We can get the chairs in the morning," I tell her as I lead us toward the streetlights to guide our short walk back to my apartment. When we hit the sidewalk, I loosen my grip in an attempt to release my hand from hers, but she holds on firmly, so I do the same.

"Do you believe in ghosts?" I ask, trying not to think too much into our drunken hand-holding.

"Sure," she replies.

"Well, the locals say there's a ghost, a little girl, five or six years old maybe." Mabel squeezes my hand tighter. I squeeze back.

"She passed away during the Civil War. Pneumonia. Anyway, it wasn't unusual at the time to see injured soldiers hobbling in and out of town in search of the hospital. One evening, while still healthy, the little girl told her parents, 'It's so dark outside, how are the soldiers going to find help?' She was likely just scared of the dark, so her parents laughed it off. But after the little girl passed, her parents put gas lanterns up through the entire town in her memory. Now, the lanterns are long gone, of course, but they say that when these streetlights flicker, that's the little girl still guiding people to their destinations."

I stop, just in front of my apartment steps, to face Mabel's reaction to the story. She smiles at me and, without a single word, grabs my other hand. My heart beats rapidly against my chest. I'm so taken aback by her forwardness, by her beauty, by the fact that she had a boyfriend five days ago and now she is holding both of my hands in both of hers.

She gently intertwines all ten of her fingers with mine. Neither of us move. I can hardly breathe.

"I liked the story, Emma." Mabel looks up from our tangled fingers, our height nearly identical, our noses so close, our eyes locked.

She releases her right hand from mine and places it gently on my cheek, brushing her fingers down my temple and wrapping them just slightly around my neck, up the back of my ear. My pulse slows, warmth floods my insides.

I don't know if it's fate, or the ghost girl, or God-sent, or a combination of all three, but the streetlight above flickers and we immediately press our foreheads together in laughter. Our hesitations disperse instantly, and our bodies compel into one another.

Mabel gently shifts her head, pressing her cheek against mine. Her skin, so smooth, smells of honeysuckle and charcoal. She grazes her lips softly, slowly down my jawline until our lips meet. A single kiss, and then another, and another.

"I've wanted to kiss you since the baseball game, Emma."

I tug her shirt, and up the concrete steps we go to my second-floor apartment, straight back to my bedroom.

I press my body against hers, shoving a faint breath from her chest as we thump against my canary-yellow bedroom door.

"You've been with women before." I know, giving my lips to her naked neck and my fingers to the buttons of her holey jeans.

"Years ago."

I step back, inhaling soberness, still trying to grasp how we got to this moment. Mabel slips off her shirt, then her bra, tossing both atop my gaudy gold floor-length mirror. She steps out of her unbuckled jeans and moves toward me.

The salty June sun waves in through the thin plastic blinds and rivers along the insides of her thighs. I pull her into me, grazing my lips down her neck, over her nipples. Her hands crawl up my stomach, lifting my shirt. She urges me toward the bed, our bare bodies pressed against one another, before she drops to her knees. I cape my fingers around her neck, gently pulling her lips into me, while she shimmies what is left of my clothing to the floor.

My legs tremble. She kisses them, me, every part of me. I hold her tighter, closer, harder, harder, until my tense grip releases, and she crawls onto the bed beside me.

I want her badly, and I know it won't take long. Her body arches toward me as I lightly stroke the inside of her thighs.

"I want you inside me," she whispers.

I listen, swallowing a moan. She breathes heavily as I slide in and out. Heavier. In and out. Until she slams her thighs shut, squeezing my hand between them with a sultry moan.

Exhaling deeply, she curls her body into mine, laying her head on my shoulder as if I were made for her.

"Mabel," I ask. "What's your full name?"

"Mabel Ann Pickett. What's yours?"

"Emma June Sloane."

"You are beautiful, Emma June."

I brush a stray curl from her face. "You are beautiful, Mabel Ann."

Monday, June 2

Lou pounces through my bedroom door. "Wake up, Emmy!" Mabel and I have slept for an hour, at most.

"Shit," Mabel mumbles, digging her face into my pillow.

"Shit!" Lou repeats, ten octaves higher. "You guys are naked."

Lou hops onto my queen-sized bed, sandwiching me between her and Mabel. Unfazed by our nudity, Lou rants, "I had no idea you were into girls, Mabel. I mean Emma is so obvious with her V-necks and those predictable Converse tennis shoes, but you, you are not so obvious."

I find Lou's rambling hilarious, but Mabel still hasn't lifted her head from my armpit, so I bite my tongue and interrupt Lou. "Don't you have work?"

Lou hops right up. "Yes I do." She skips out of the room shouting, "I can't wait to go on double dates with you guys."

Mabel lifts her head, rubbing the tired from her eyes. "That went well."

"Better than some coming-out stories." I smile, rolling out from under the linen duvet. "Do you drink coffee?" I ask while slipping on a baggy white T-shirt and an oversized pair of gray sweatpants.

"Yes."

Thank God. Coffee and beer are nonnegotiables for me. There's no logical reason behind that thinking other than I like coffee and I like beer and I want to share these little joys with whomever I wake up naked next to.

"Cream?"

She doesn't hesitate. "Black."

Bold. Even better.

I toss her a gray "Shepherd Women's Basketball" T-shirt, one of dozens, and a pair of navy mesh basketball shorts before heading to the kitchen.

"You slept with her," Lou says, popping her head up from the open fridge.

"Lou!" I say, shushing her with my finger. "I thought you left."

"I didn't and I want to know how that," she says, nodding toward the bedroom, "happened."

"I'm not sure." My cheeks redden. I have no idea how it happened, but I'm pretty giddy about it and Louie can tell.

"Awe, Emmy," she whispers, shutting the fridge. "You are welcome for the introduction."

I lift Lou's mud-stained blue Patagonia bag from the floor and shove it into her arms. "Thank you," I murmur, urging her toward the front door.

* * *

"Here you go," I say, handing Mabel a stolen Betty's Diner mug filled to the brim. "It's a hazelnut blend. Hope you like it." Her hair is in the same braid from last night, except a bit more frazzled. Her skin glows of summer.

"Perfect." She smiles, cradling the warm mug in her two hands. I crawl back into bed beside her, our backs against the flattened pillows, the pillows against the cold vinyl wallpaper.

I look around the room, noticing, for the first time, that there isn't much to distract us. I have a bulky television that sits atop a hand-me-down wooden desk, the same desk that my mother used as a child. A large pinned-up map of the Appalachian Trail hangs on an otherwise empty wall just left of the door, and a thirsty pothos vine curls over the windowsill.

"So, you've been with women before?" I ask, hoping I'm not crossing any lines.

Her lips curl into a half-moon smile, shifting her left eye into a squinty rainbow as she remembers spilling this bit of information during our tango.

"One woman," she clarifies.

"Only one? Will you tell me about her?"

"I was sixteen. So was she. We were friends. Great friends. Things just escalated."

"That's it?" I probe.

She laughs and continues, "Well, we'd stay up all night. Like most teenagers do, you know. Some nights we'd steal a shot or two of her dad's liquor; just enough to justify our attraction." She smiles at the vivid recollection. "The first time we kissed was in her ninety-one Honda Civic. That car was such a piece of shit. We had snuck out and we were driving around, further than normal, taking windy roads, looking for quiet. She stopped the car when she found an empty cove by a cornfield and she kissed me, like she had been planning the moment for months." Mabel snaps out of her memory. "And that's really how it started."

"Romantic." I smirk, oddly jealous of her intimate memories with someone I would never know.

"It kind of was."

"Then what happened?"

"Gosh." She exhales. "I've wished it away enough that I can hardly remember." She takes a deep breath, her hands still cupped around her coffee mug. "She had written me something mushy, a love note, in school one day. This girl, Stephanie Ratcliff, found it. What a bully. It must have fallen out of my locker or my backpack. Who knows, but Stephanie outed us to the entire school." Mabel shrugs her shoulders. "It was this...this whole thing. The principal called my parents and her parents. Ugh. It was awful. That was it for me. I could not be with a girl."

"Do you talk to her still?" I ask. "Your friend?"

"No. Not at all. We spoke a few times after it all went down, but my parents kept asking me about her and I just wasn't ready to handle all of it. So, I denied it, endlessly, and I shut her out of my life. Pretended like nothing ever happened." Her cheeks are flushed, still embarrassed maybe, after all this time. "It's pathetic, I know."

"It's not pathetic," I say, finding it difficult to muster up a more comforting response.

"I assume that your coming-out story was a little less dramatic," she says, taking a sip of coffee.

"It was definitely…different." I nod.

"Go ahead, spill."

"Well, this is a lot for our first coffee date," I say. "But since we've already been naked together, I'll share."

Mabel nods her head in a way that insinuates it was absolutely time for me to share something extremely personal because, why not?

"My mom actually passed away from breast cancer when I was eleven and she left me a letter to open on my eighteenth birthday." I reach into my nightstand and pull out a neatly folded piece of paper. "It's…it's right here," I stutter as I carefully unfold it.

Though I've nearly memorized it, I read one of the paragraphs verbatim:

"Marry someone who is kind and will light the Shabbat candles with you on Friday nights. If you don't want to marry, don't. If you don't want to light the candles, don't. Just be happy. Choose happiness, above all else, always. Drink beer. Not too much. Watch baseball. Grow sunflowers. Be in love. Love rules. And life is good. Life is real, real good. Remember that, will ya? You, Emma June, are gonna be great. PS. Light the candles."

I notice Mabel's eyes are misting as I fold up the letter. "She didn't specify 'man' in her letter when referring to marriage, and that was really all the approval I needed to come out to my dad. But before I could even spit it out to him, he pulled me in for a hug and told me that he had read more than one of my love notes." I chuckle aloud at the memory. "I was so embarrassed."

"Both of your parents sound wonderful," Mabel says, her eyes locked on mine.

"Yes. She was. He is."

Wednesday, June 11

"Hello, Emma."

"Hi!" My heart picks up pace instantly as I hastily brush clean the powdered sugar and pastry crumbles from my apron. "What are you doing here?"

"I'm here to get a coffee." Mabel smiles, scanning the pastry selection before pointing to a neatly stacked pile of cinnamon-roll rugelach. "And one of those."

I hand her the rugelach and an empty coffee cup for her to fill at the adjacent coffee station. "Here, take it, on me. Is that all you want?"

As she fills it up, she asks, "Well, I was wondering if you'd like to walk up to that Rumsey Monument you were telling me about last night?"

During our phone call last night, she told me that her favorite color is Crayola's Blue Lagoon and that she doesn't like ketchup, or pineapple pizza. I told her that I keep a journal, but it's more like a notebook of poetic chicken scratch. And I told her that I like the color yellow and that we should go to the Rumsey Monument on Friday when she comes over.

It's only Wednesday.

I have been aching for this sloth of a week to hurry along so I could touch her velvet skin again, but here she is. Two days early, sporting a golden Washington Redskins cap and a pair of Danner hiking boots with bright red laces.

"Does this mean I still get to see you on Friday?"

"I already can't wait," she assures.

The church bells ring three times, lifting both of our eyebrows in eagerness. I slip off my apron, clock out, and off we go.

The Rumsey Monument sits high above the Potomac River on the edge of downtown. It was built in the early nineteen hundreds as a tribute to James Rumsey, the inventor of the steamboat. Of course, most that enjoy the monument's memorial park have no idea who James Rumsey is, nor do they care why he deserves a monument.

I learned the fun fact during my English 101 class, so I share it with Mabel as we walk down the street, around the river bend, and up the hill to the park.

We take a seat on the back side of the statue, using its shade to hide from the midafternoon sun. The Norfolk Southern train sails by over the Potomac and we count each rusty cart as it passes. Fifty-six and a caboose.

"What's your favorite holiday tradition?" Mabel asks.

Despite our excessive amounts of phone calls and texts since she left my bed on Monday morning, the discovery continues.

"Tough," I say, leaning my back against the cool concrete ledge. "I think it's Shabbat. Few and far between since college, but growing up, most Friday nights we did Shabbat. Lit the candles, said the prayers, all that good stuff. It's just a simple holiday. An opportunity to reflect on the week. And it reminds me of my mom."

"How so?"

"She loved Shabbat. She'd cook massive meals. Mashed coconut sweet potatoes and grilled asparagus and brisket that simmered sunrise to set. She'd invite her brother over, my Uncle Joey, and we'd play card games or do a puzzle or watch a movie together. I've probably romanticized it all over the years, but they're good memories."

Mabel sits on the ledge just below me, tracing the lines on my outstretched palm with her pointer finger, smiling at my memoirs.

"So, you're pretty Jewish?"

I chuckle. "I'm Jewishy."

"Was that offensive to ask?" She covers her hand over her mouth, her eyes widening.

"It's not! It's not at all," I assure her.

"Well, what does Jewishy mean then?"

"Well, I guess, it's the culture and the tradition I really enjoy."

"So that just makes ya Jewish, doesn't it?"

"Well, yeah, but maybe not as much as the ones that actually go to synagogue and pray."

She giggles softly.

"What?" I also chuckle, not because I know what she's laughing at, but because I find her raspy, deep giggle so cute it makes me happy.

"Well, that's just silly," she insists, leaning in to kiss my forehead as if she had done it a million times before.

"Yeah." I smile. "I guess it is. Anyway, it's your turn. What's your favorite holiday tradition?"

"Cookies. Eating excessive amounts of cookies is always acceptable at the holidays. Oatmeal raisin on Easter. Turkey-shaped sugar cookies at Thanksgiving. Molasses cookies and gingerbread men with cute little chocolate chip buttons on Christmas." I belly laugh at the pure joy in her face. "I'm serious!" she cries. "My brother, AJ, and I demolish them. Every holiday. It's a competition. My absolute favorite tradition is to eat all the cookies."

"Well, do you bake them or buy them?"

"We bake them, of course. But I don't necessarily enjoy that part of the tradition. It's more of a necessity. Ya know, to get to the good part."

Journal: Thursday, June 12, 2008

She's like fresh sheets.
Sunshine.
Like a Sunday,
when you don't have a single place in the entire world to be.

Thursday, June 12

Mine and Lou's old apartment window units are set at sixty-eight and pushing seventy-five at best. They are no match for June, so we head downtown to the Blue Moon Café for relief and lunch. We sit at a wooden table near the back of the restaurant and order two black teas on ice.

I'm distracted with thoughts of the morning, peeling my skin from Mabel's before the sun rose. Her tired laugh. Her lips against my cheek as she said, "See ya, Emma June."

Lou interrupts my daydreams with her timeless humor. "You are head over Converses for her, Emmy!"

I laugh at how pitifully smitten I am.

"Just be careful," Lou warns as she dumps brown sugar packets into her tea. "She is wonderful. You know that I think she is great, but you're my number one. Max said that Jack is still pretty torn up over their breakup and you know, he's probably trying to get her back."

It hasn't even been a month since Mabel and Jack split. Of course Jack is struggling. Mabel probably is too. How naive of me to think that I could be anything more than a rebound for Mabel.

"Did Max say that Jack and Mabel had been talking?" I hope I haven't sounded too desperately curious, but I am.

"Jack mentioned to Max that they had spoken. Could have been nothing, though. Max didn't ask details. You know how he is."

"Quiet? Boring? The worst gossiper of all time?"

"Exactly," Lou confirms.

I stir my straw around the ice cubes in my glass. "It's nothing serious anyway," I share, peering out the window. The typically lush gardens out back are spotted with yellow stains, and all the neighborhood cats are lying under the willowing oak tree, dabbing their paws in the koi pond. "It's a summer thing. That's all."

Journal: Friday, June 13, 2008

I gave her my umbrella.
As long as she is weathering her storm, she'll want it.
I should take it back now. Keep myself dry and warm and safe.
But the rain feels so nice on my skin.

Friday, June 13

Mabel walks into the apartment carrying warm challah bread and wildflowers. "Jewishy people eat challah bread on Shabbat, right?" She places the bouquet on the kitchen counter and lifts a bottle of pinot noir from her overnight duffel.

The thoughtfulness pushes yesterday's conversation with Louie aside. I pull Mabel into me and hug her tightly. "Thank you."

I hustle back to my bedroom and grab two gold candlesticks from the top shelf in my closet. "These were my mom's," I tell her, before guiding her out to the back deck and placing them on the patio table. "This is the first time I've used them since I left for school."

"The first time?" Her eyes curl up with her lips. "I'm honored. And look at this. Mushroom risotto?"

I nod. "Is that all right?"

"Yes! Of course." She smiles. "It looks delicious."

I smile, pleased with her response. "Sit, sit," I tell her.

I light the candles and say the blessings for the candles, the wine, and the bread, in Hebrew without hiccup.

"Growing up, we had a Shabbat tradition to share one bad thing from our week and one good thing from our week," I tell Mabel. "The bad we share to release, and the good we carry with us into the new week."

If she thinks it's silly, she's doing a good job of hiding it.

"I like that," she says, swirling the red wine in her stemless glass. She's wearing a mustard-yellow sundress and chestnut-colored sandals with thick leather straps. Her hair hangs in loose spirals, frizzy from humidity. Her freckles are darkened by the long sun-filled days of June.

"You," she says, "have brought me an immeasurable amount of joy this week. You're my good thing. And as far as my bad thing goes…" She hesitates. "I have already thought too often about how short the summer is." She squints her eyes in question. "Can't really get rid of the end of summer, though, can we?"

"No," I say, smiling gently. "Can't get rid of that."

I take a small sip of wine, digesting her response. I've thought about it too. The end of summer. How the brilliance of a firework never lasts. I let my conversation with Louie creep back in.

"So, you're doing all right?" I ask. "Ya know, with the breakup and all?"

Mabel looks up from her wine. Appearing to look confused. Probably wondering why I've just disrupted our evening with some seriously unnecessary question about Jack.

My shoulders and neck stiffen. I'm annoyed at myself for not just minding my own business.

"I, uh…" She shakes her head side to side, softly swirling her wine again. "I haven't thought about it much."

I take a sip to avoid having to muster up a reply.

She continues, "I'm just…I'm just really enjoying this summer. Jack and I, ya know, we weren't happy. I'm happy right now."

She lifts her glass up for a *cheers*. "To the happiest of summers."

My insides warm, and I feel the tension in my body release with a smile. "To the happiest of summers," I repeat.

JULY

Monday, July 7

"I made this for you at work today," Mabel says, handing over a piece of four-by-six, thick card stock.

Mabel left River Rat's Rafting to work as the receptionist of her mother's art gallery and studio in downtown Frederick. The shop typically only drives weekend business, but she pays Mabel eight bucks an hour to handle the minimal weekday traffic and maintain the pristine cleaning. Her mother takes the wheel on most weekends, opening day of new exhibits, and any special events.

I checked out the current exhibit early last week. It's titled "America" and features the mixed-media work of a single West Virginia artist that specializes in small-town landscapes such as a trailer park gathering in Shepherdsville, Kentucky; a soda fountain in Pella, Iowa; a book cubby in a rainy Winthrop, Washington forest. Fifty paintings, one for each state.

"It was a slow day." Mabel smirks. She says this nearly every day.

The postcard-sized artwork depicts an outline, drawn in pencil, of two women tangled together, their lips touching.

Their bodies water-colored in native wildflowers: black-eyed Susans, bright purple lupines, and butterfly weed.

"Mae, this is amazing," I exclaim, sincerely impressed. "The detail, the color. It's brilliant! I had no idea you were so artistic."

Her cheeks blush. "It's just a hobby. I'm glad you like it."

I dig through the back of my bedroom closet, keeper of all hidden goods, and pull out a four-by-six weathered white wooden frame. "I knew I hung on to this for something special." I wink.

Mabel nods. "Well, that's convenient."

I carefully place the drawing in the frame. "I'm not sure if our bodies are capable of twisting like this," I say as I use a pushpin to hang the picture up above my nightstand.

She laughs and steps toward me, lifting off her shirt. "We should try, though, huh?"

Wednesday, July 16

I hurry down the apartment steps as Mabel whips around the block. I heard her rickety 1985 forest-green Ford Ranger revving up a half mile down the road. It was her dad's farm truck at one time, but he put a radio in it, fixed the dents, most of them anyway, and gave it to her on her seventeenth birthday.

She loves her truck.

I open the rigid passenger door and hop in. We're heading to an afternoon at the batting cages.

"I want to know more about your mom," Mabel says.

I reach for a Polaroid dated March 1987 in my wallet and hand it to Mabel. "That's my mom and my dad on their wedding day."

The sepia-toned picture features my mom in a white flowy dress. It's hanging loosely over her very pregnant belly. A flower crown sits atop layers of dark hair. Her face is glowing.

My father is much taller than my mother. Lean with broad shoulders. He's sporting fitted khaki pants, suspenders, and a navy bow tie. They're a handsome couple.

"She looks just like you."

"Yeah." I nod. "My dad always says that." I kick my legs up on the dashboard, printing my bare toes on the windshield. "Minus the belly of course, right?" I chuckle.

"Right." She winks. "How did they meet?" Mabel asks, handing the picture back.

"They were high school sweethearts, actually. They grew up in Alexandria, Virginia. That's where my dad still lives. After high school, my dad got drafted to the Pittsfield Cubs, a double-A affiliate of the Chicago Cubs. They're not even around anymore."

"No way! What position?" Mabel seems elated at this discovery.

"Second base." I smile proudly. "My mom followed him to Pittsfield, Massachusetts. She was working at a diner and going to school, and he was playing baseball, and all of that was super short-lived because they got pregnant with me and moved right on back to Virginia."

We both laugh.

"I was probably a mistake, huh?"

"Their best one," Mabel assures.

"You want to meet him?" I ask. "My dad?" My heart drops the second the words leave my mouth. It's too much, too soon. I desperately wish I could reel the words back in.

"Yes," she says without hesitation. "I would love that."

Journal: Thursday, July 17, 2008

Going
Going
Gone.

Saturday, July 19

Mabel waves from the white picket fence and I hurry over to let her into the backyard of my childhood home.

"Hi!" I hope my joy is apparent in my wide grin.

"Hi." She smiles before leaning in to kiss my cheek.

I grab her hand and we scurry over to my dad. He's grilling burgers and boiling corn. Listening intently to the Orioles game that is blaring through the screen door.

"These are for you, Mr. Sloane," Mabel says as he looks up to greet her. She hands over a bundle of perky yellow sunflowers.

"Call me Barry." He smiles. "And thank you so much, Miss Mabel." He heads inside for a vase.

"Thanks for coming," I whisper in Mabel's ear. She had to work for a few hours at the gallery this morning, so we drove separately.

"I'm happy to be here," Mabel says, following my dad inside.

"Emma must have told you that these were her mother's favorite flowers?"

"I didn't," I chime in.

My dad looks up from the kitchen sink with a raise of his eyebrows, clearly pleased. He meticulously cuts each sunflower to the length he prefers and spruces them up in a tall glass vase before stepping back to admire his efficient work.

"I don't have them in the house nearly enough. Feels more like home now, doesn't it, Em?"

I smile and squeeze Mabel's hand. "That was very sweet of you."

"You guys ready to pop open a few of my newest beers?" my dad asks.

He and a couple of his neighborhood buddies went to Oktoberfest in Germany when I was in middle school. The three of them came back to the States fired up on home brewing. Dad portioned off a section of our garage, managed to find a twenty-gallon and a seven-gallon copper kettle through an antique dealer in Lancaster, Pennsylvania and has been brewing up boatloads of bizarre concoctions ever since. I've been a part of the madness from day one. He even let me have a small sip of beer after each batch, which I gagged at until I was well into my freshman year of college.

I grab three brown-bottled crisp hoppy ales from the beer fridge in the garage while my dad places a tray of burgers, corn, and sweet potato fries on the kitchen counter.

"Good choice, Em. A hint of honey in these bad boys. Kinda like the ones you and I brewed last summer, actually."

Mabel looks impressed. "You can make beer as well, Emma?"

Before I can answer, Dad chimes in. "Yeah, she can! Has a real knack for it. Been doing it long before she could even drink it."

I roll my eyes at him to assure Mabel he's exaggerating. The three of us crack open the beers and take our seats.

"You taste the honey in there?" Dad asks.

It does carry a mellow sweetness, I'm just not sure it's the honey that I taste, but I wouldn't dare be honest because he cares too much about this side hobby of his. "I do." I nod.

"Good." He grins. "I'm still looking forward to the day you open up your own brewery so we can do a dad-daughter duo brew." He winks at his cheesy request.

"One day," I assure.

Mabel looks over at me with a curious side smile, probably wondering why I haven't, in our endless hours of talk, shared this aspiration.

"It's a dream," I tell her. "We'll see what happens."

"It's an awesome dream," she declares. "I look forward to trying your beers one day."

I see Dad smile at Mabel's enthusiasm before addressing her. "Mabel, what are you studying?"

I can't imagine what Dad is thinking. I've never brought a girl home for him to meet before, and I'm feeling slightly insane for bringing one that I've known for less than two months.

"I'm majoring in political science. Though I have no idea what I want to do. Maybe teach?"

I know my dad is thrilled. He also did his undergraduate studies in Poli-Sci.

His perky smile widens. "Have you considered law?"

Her eyebrows raise. She's intrigued. "I actually have been toying with the idea of it. It's the three years of student loans I'm not crazy about."

"Don't get him started, Mae. He's a lawyer."

She ignores me and asks, "What kind of law do you practice?"

He proceeds to tell her all about his humble beginnings and how he started his own firm back in 2001 providing affordable legal services to immigrants and refugees. He tackles everything from petty crimes to green cards and citizenship.

"It's a fulfilling line of work," he says. "The loans are overwhelming. I understand. But the industry is fruitful, and if you live modestly, you'll knock it out in a decade." His bushy eyebrows raise. "Maybe sooner."

What was supposed to be an afternoon of baseball evolves into an evening of rich laughter, conversation, and a few too many beers. Mabel and I fall asleep on the living room couch and wake up to my dad hustling out to meet his Sunday morning biking team.

"Girls, there's coffee made. Help yourself."

He kisses my forehead and whispers, "I like her, Emma June."

Mabel sits up from the couch. "Thanks for having me, Barry. I'll give law school some more thought."

"You'll let me know if you have any questions." He winks before heading out the front door.

When the lock clicks, Mabel stands, stretching and shaking the tired from her body. "Can I see your room?"

"Sure." I roll up from the couch and lead her down the wooden hallway toward the stairs. The smell of jasmine wafts in through the windows, and I remember how my mom used to love the way the vines danced around the columns on the front porch.

Despite the "Do Not Enter" sign that's been hanging on my bedroom door since seventh grade, I turn the knob and push it open. It's still a pale yellow from when my dad and I painted it on my thirteenth birthday. The large wall along the back wears two black-framed posters. One of Sue Bird in a Huskies uniform and another of Kobe Bryant in a purple Lakers jersey. Dozens of ribbons and plastic trophies fill the three wide shelves perpendicular to the posters and a few old stuffed bears sit beneath them. On my square nightstand beside my double bed is a picture of my mom and me on the front steps. I remember the day clearly. I had just run through the sprinkler, hair wet and tangled. I must have been five or six at the time. I'm sitting between her legs. Her arms wrapped tightly around me. Both of us full of joy. It's one of my favorite pictures of the two of us.

"That's a really nice picture," Mabel says, noticing that our attention is on the same photo. "Look at you. So cute." She plops down on the bed. "Looks the same?" she asks.

"Exactly the same."

"Mine is too." She smiles before asking, "Have you ever brought someone home before?"

"Someone? Yes, but someone that I like? No. You are the first."

"You like me?" Her eyes widen in delight, already knowing the answer.

"I do," I confirm as she motions for me to come closer. I gently lay her down onto the bed, crawl on top, and steady my hips against hers before kissing her softly. Letting her magic cast spells through every bone in my body. I lift my lips just inches from hers to grab hold of her gentle eyes. "I like you a lot."

Journal: Sunday, July 20, 2008

I think I'd like her around long after the summer ends.

Saturday, July 26

"It was so great meeting your dad last weekend." Mabel huffs as we round the rugged hike toward Chimney Rock vista.

"I'm glad you came."

"He sparked my interest in law," she says. "Can't stop thinking about the opportunities now."

I'm not surprised by Mabel's sudden urge to explore the opportunities within law. My dad reeks of passion when he discusses his career.

"When he was talking about his firm," she begins. "All the people he's helped, the real impact he's had on families. That's what I wanna do...ya know...make a real difference."

"I'm sure you will, regardless of what you do." I smile at her, happy that she enjoyed the visit with him as much as I did.

"Oh, you're just being nice."

I'm not, but she can think that. "A little, maybe."

She offers a quick grin before asking, "Wanna stop for a bit before we loop back?"

I nod, and we maneuver our way onto the rocky summit to find a flat surface to sit down on. I lug the backpack cooler from my shoulders and pull out two of my dad's crispy cold Apple Ales for us to enjoy.

"Do I get to meet your family at some point?" I ask as we pop open the bottles.

I only asked to spark conversation, but the way her eyes divert from mine tells me she's stunned by the question. My chest tightens at the unexpected response.

"Someday, maybe."

Ouch. "You haven't told them a thing about us, huh?"

"Not yet." She shrugs.

"Not yet, or not ever?" I ask, forcing a chuckle, though it's ingenuine. We've never established any official commitment, so I'm hesitant to be too assertive with my desires.

"Oh, stop." She smiles, pulling my hand into her lap and holding it tight.

Oh, stop? Stop what? This?

I stare at our hands, her fingers laced with mine, feeling silly for allowing myself to get too connected.

"Look there." She points at a bald eagle circling above the towering pines. "Amazing, isn't she?"

I inhale the deep mountain laurels and breathe out the blatant disregard of my question and the inadvertent trampling of my emotions.

My exhale, louder than intended, along with my lack of response, causes her to shift her attention toward me. "You see her?" she asks, a bit softer this time, as she tightens her grip on my hand.

"How do you know she's a she?" I ask, avoiding eye contact.

I feel her look away. "She's strong. The females are bigger, wider wingspan. It's tough to tell sometimes, but this one…she's beautiful."

Journal: Sunday, July 26, 2008

She picked up a rock from the bank,
watched it dance along the crystal blue glass.
A captivating ballerina.
She picked up another.
And another.
And the bank looks a little bare now.
Does it feel lighter?
Or just empty?
Either way, it isn't what it once was.

Thursday, July 31

"Let's do it, ladies and gent!" Louie barks in her assertive River Rat's guide voice.

Lou, Max, Mabel, and I hop to attention. We're taking a sunset stroll down the river. Since Louie is managing the team of river guides this season, she purposefully scheduled the last rafting group of the night to set out twenty minutes earlier than usual so that the four of us could enjoy a quiet, secluded float.

Since Louie hooked us up with the free life jackets and tubes, Mabel and I brought the twelve-pack of Bud Light.

"Look at us out here livin' the dream!" Louie sings as she lounges back in her tube, both of her arms drifting beneath the cool water. She's in her element.

"This really is the dream, Em, huh?" Mabel is wading her toes up and down in the water, chipper as a toddler in a splash park.

I chuckle in agreement as I scan up the bark of the towering sycamore trees and back down to the subtle rapids that are gossiping in small pods amongst the rocks.

Mabel lassos a rope onto my tube so we can float within an arm's length of each other. "It's pretty great," I tell her, reaching for her hand.

"Tell me more about this brewery you want to open."

"I like the idea of opening a small spot. Maybe here in Harpers Ferry. Or Shepherdstown."

"Or Frederick!" Mabel chimes in.

I smile. I imagine a brick brewery along Carroll Creek in Frederick, somewhere near the art gallery that Mabel's mom owns. An open garage door that flows from the taproom to the outdoor patio. A firepit for the cool autumn nights, black iron tables and chairs. Families gathered around empty pint glasses. Abundant laughter. Conversations roaring.

"Yeah, Frederick would be awesome," I confirm. "Wherever it ends up being, though, I just like the idea of owning my own business. Having the creative liberty to brew whatever I'm feeling. Determining my own success."

She looks impressed with my strewn dream. "It's going to be wonderful," Mabel declares confidently.

"Time for cheesy jokes!" Max shouts, grabbing our attention. Within a few moments, Mabel and Max are in a laugh battle. I loosen the rope from Mabel's tube and paddle over toward Louie to chat.

"You two really have something special," Lou whispers.

The sun has started to decline, stretching its soft mint arms across the horizon. I let Mabel's aura wash over me before responding.

"This has been the absolute best summer of my life," I tell Lou. "But I dunno what's gonna happen. You know, she's not out yet. Not to her family, not to her friends. No one, but us."

"Maybe she's not ready yet. Give her time."

"Well." I look down at the date on my waterproof watch. "She's got about three weeks before she heads back to school."

"That doesn't mean anything. Plenty of people figure things out from afar."

"I know. I know, but this is different. She's got a whole life down in North Carolina. Friends that know Jack. That may think they're still together. That definitely don't think she's interested in women. I could just be a summer thing for her. Something she'll move on from as soon as she gets back to school."

"You are not just a summer thing. That, if nothing else, is clear as this day."

I smile softly at Lou, appreciating her perception.

"I think I've gotten too caught up in the formalities of our relationship."

"That's because you like her!"

"I do." I giggle. "Gosh. I need to take a step back, huh? Just enjoy her...us...for what it is."

Lou ponders my contemplation for a moment. "Well, ya better go enjoy," she urges with a wink before nudging my tube back over toward Mabel. "The summer is tickin' away."

AUGUST

Journal: Friday, August 1, 2008

I'm not sure I believe in love at first sight.
I think it's a compilation of moments.
Moments that build,
the truck ride, the sunset, the clothes sprawled across the floor.
And build,
her lips, the blinds, her voice, the heat.
And build up in your soul until you are no longer the you that was
you before her.
And it'll happen without notice.
Right there in the middle of the river.
On a mint green Thursday evening.
A cheap cold beer in her hand.
A smile that could melt the entire sea.
"That's her. She is the one that I love."

Monday, August 18

The sun is tiptoeing below the water. We're lying atop a cerulean wool blanket on Chincoteague Island, knee-deep in tequila. Mabel drove over from Ocean City, Maryland where she spent a long weekend vacationing with her family. I drove the three hours down from Shepherdstown with a tent, peanut butter and jelly sandwiches, and, of course, the tequila.

Just for the evening, just to see her.

"Do you think your parents would care that you're hanging out with me?" I ask.

Our conversation during our Chimney Rock hike has been lurking over me for the last few weeks, and as our summer closes, I find myself with an innate need to know that I'm important to her. That I'm more than just a summer fling.

"I'm not sure," she responds.

"You're not sure? I'm a female. Would they like that you are sleeping with a female?"

"I don't think they want me to be sleeping with anyone."

Good point. "Who do your parents think you met here today?"

"Some friends."

Her lack of interest is frustrating me. "Not a word about me yet, huh?"

"No," she confirms, shaking her head. "I'm sorry."

We sit quiet for a few moments. I feel defeated by the failed conversation and the impending end of summer.

She inhales deeply. "They wouldn't get it. I don't think."

"You wouldn't know," I say calmly but firmly. "You haven't given them the opportunity to understand."

"You're right, I guess, but I don't even get it. I mean, I get it, but it's a lot to digest. My family, my friends, they know me with Jack. I started this summer dating a man and I'm ending it with you."

My throat drops deep in my gut, all her words sinking me. I recall my conversation at Blue Moon Diner with Lou back in June. I should have scaled back my feelings then. I should have known I was nothing more than a rebound for Mabel. That this was nothing more than a silly summer fling.

"I get it—it's hard," I lie, gulping back my self-worth, trying desperately not to let the swelling tears in my eyes fall.

She continues, "A week from now, I'll be back at school. You'll carry on here…with your life, and your friends, and your senior year."

"It doesn't have to be like that," I push.

"But it's going to be like that."

I stop responding, for fear of breaking down completely. We watch the sky paint itself pink, and then orange, and then dark, dark blue, until we crawl into our tent.

The backs of our hands are touching and we're peering through the unzipped tent roof at the dim stars overhead. Through the silence, I replay our summer. The ribbons I scratched into her back last Tuesday morning. The day I left her a sidewalk chalk message on the stairs up to my apartment door. June twenty-fifth, when I counted the twenty-four freckles on her nose and cheeks. And June twenty-sixth, when she said, "You make me very happy, Emma June," while we danced to Tim McGraw's "When the Stars go Blue."

All of that feels pretty distant right now, like we're already miles away from each other.

Tuesday, August 19

We wake with the sun. Mabel asks me to lie on the beach with her a while, but I tell her I have to go to work.

It's a lie. She knows that.

I took the day off with the intention to spend every possible minute within her reach, but my head is pounding from tequila and our dead-end conversation.

We stand face-to-face. I beg her silently to tell me that she loves me, that she'll tell the world about us, that she wants to try to make this work despite the distance.

Her weary eyes tell me that she hears me, that she's sorry, that she knows she has hurt me, but she wants me to think less about the future and more about what Pandora playlist we can listen to while we watch the morning mist rise off the ocean.

"You sure you can't stay?" she asks, her voice raspy, defeated.

"Not today." We pack up the tent in silence and toss it into the back of my car. A quick kiss on the cheek sends me on my way. The endless soybean farms lining Route 50 offer no reprieve for my swollen eyes.

This is the end.

Summer is over.

Mabel will be heading back to North Carolina, and I'll be staying in Shepherdstown drinking the same breakfast blend coffee from the Sweet Shoppe Bakery.

Every. Single. Cup. Will make me think of her.

I'll lie down in my bed tonight and tomorrow night and next month, and I'll imagine her snuggling up behind me in the middle of the night, kissing my neck before dozing back off to sleep. Every trail we hiked will remind me of her. Every rattling green truck, every wildflower. Every single summer, maybe forever, will make me think of her.

Mabel Ann Pickett.

I call Alli, knowing as I dial her number that tomorrow morning I will not only feel more sad than I do now, but also ashamed and disappointed with myself.

I meet her at two in the basement bar at Tony's Pizza. We drink five-dollar pitchers and two-dollar shooters until we've lost all sense of responsibility. I kiss her neck. I think of Mabel. We go back to her place. I turn off my phone. I rip off her clothes. We shower together. We sleep naked.

Journal: Wednesday, August 20, 2008

There was more to us,
so I squeezed all the feeling from her love notes while I slept.
Now there is nothing more to us,
except the ink stains on my pillow.

Friday, August 22

"I know it's early," Mabel says.

The very sight of her sends prickles up my arms. I grip the side of the doorframe to prevent myself from draping my sleepy arms around her before nearly whispering, "It's five a.m., Mabel. It's the earliest I've woken up all summer."

"Oh, stop it." She chuckles with energy as if it's the middle of the day. "We've stayed up until this hour many times."

I try not to look amused.

"Here, I brought you coffee."

I take the teal UNCW thermos from her. "That's a start," I say, pleased with the scent of hazelnut. I commend myself for acting unfazed.

We haven't spoken since our camping trip to Chincoteague Island. Not a single word. Not a text or a call. Nothing since Tuesday morning. I spent most of Wednesday regretting Tuesday night with Alli and most of Thursday staring at my bedroom ceiling, trying desperately to ignore the pit in the bottom of my throat.

"I'm leaving this afternoon for school," she says. "Will you come out on the canoe with me? Please."

"Yes."

＊ ＊ ＊

We push off and row a quarter mile upstream as the steam lifts with the morning.

I can't take my eyes off her. Her loosely braided hair hangs over her shoulder, just as it did on that very first afternoon when we met at Pickle's Pub in Baltimore. She has on the same golden Redskins cap that she wore on the afternoon that she surprised me at the Sweet Shoppe. Her skin, honey glazed from our long sunny days together. Her freckles, prominent, even in the dim morning mist.

"This was the best summer of my life, Mabel."

"It was the best summer of mine, Emma June."

We don't mention Chincoteague. She never asks why I didn't call. We don't talk about *us* at all.

Instead, we talk about the Orioles. "You saw Adam Jones's grand slam the other night?"

"Yeah," I tell her, smiling at the way baseball makes her face light up. "The Os sure made out with that trade."

We talk about our senior year course loads and my last collegiate basketball season. We talk about Lou and Max, how we think they'll be together forever. She asks me to send her the Sweet Shoppe's fall recipes, and I ask her to catch one of my home basketball games if she comes back to the area for Thanksgiving break.

When the river starts to fill with amateur fly-fishers, we row in to shore and load the canoe back into her truck. The early sun streams in, highlighting my bare footprints that are still stamped all over the passenger-side windshield—memories from our summer that she'll soon wash away.

"Here," she says, reaching into her hoodie pocket as she drives back into town. "I wrote you something."

I take the folded lined paper from her.

"Read it later, when you have time," she tells me.

I grab her hand from her lap and hold it tight until we get back to my apartment. Unsure if later, or never, or soon is appropriate, I kiss her hand—one last taste of her skin on my lips. "See ya, Mae."

My eyes ache as I hurry up the stairs. I don't watch her drive away, or even look back for a last wave goodbye. I shut the front door and let my entire body fall against it as I sink to the floor. Taking deep conscious breaths, I unfold her letter.

In July, that night when we sat on that concrete block ledge in town, when all the stars were out, you told me that your favorite song was "Mr. Jones" by the Counting Crows. I asked you why and you sang, "cause we all want something beautiful" and you kissed me while we were both laughing and I thought, in that moment, that I've never known a more beautiful person than you.

I hope to one day be as sure of myself as you are, Emma June.

I bought the Counting Crows CD the other night, August and Everything After. I'm going to listen to it on my drive south. I'll think of you. Your soft hands on my skin. The mornings I brushed your hair from your face. My sweetest summer.

Perhaps when timing is better, we'll meet again.

Until then,

Mae

SEPTEMBER

Journal: Monday, September 8, 2008

She'll greet you at the town's fair.
A red ribbon in her hair.
She'll ask ya, "Wanna buy a raffle, Honey?"
And you do,
because her smile makes you believe that you're the lucky one.

Journal: Tuesday, September 16, 2008

Sunday Market.
Dirty hands.
A bright white crew neck tucked into her ripped jeans.
"I'll take those," I tell her, pointing to the vase of wildflowers.
"They're beautiful, aren't they?" she asks, catching me with her seaweed eyes as she wraps tweed around the stems.
I think, my gosh, you are the most beautiful.
"They are," the next in line shouts.

Journal: Thursday, September 25, 2008

She'll leave in the middle of night.
Take the spare key and start the coffeepot on her way out.
Maybe she just went for a walk?
Gosh, this coffee is good.
Maybe she's never coming home?

OCTOBER

Journal: Wednesday, October 1, 2008

Despite every other thing being just dandy,
I miss her so deeply that it all just feels like hell.

Friday, October 10

Max and I see her at the same time. "What a babe," we whisper simultaneously, followed by an elbow from Lou for each of us. "A little class, please," Lou murmurs. "You animals."

Harsh.

We're at the men's basketball house attending their yearly season kickoff party. I like to refer to the celebration as the death of our social life. Our very last collegiate basketball season starts Monday, and for the next five or so months, Lou and I won't be attending any gatherings unless they include weights, a basketball court, or a dark classroom for scouting film.

"Who is that?" I ask. She's tall, five-eleven, maybe taller. Lean, solid, definitely an athlete.

"Kate is her name," Lou says. Of course Lou, campus's most popular socialite, knows her. "Max, you should know her," Lou continues. "She's on the women's soccer team." Lou looks at Max like he is clueless. "She's the goalie."

Max is the goalie on the men's squad. "You're right, I should go get to know her." He chuckles, teasing Lou. Their playful love is envy-worthy.

"I'm going to talk to her," I say.

Max immediately rebuts, rubbing his hand through his freshly shaven head. "No way she's into chicks."

Lou again flails her elbow, but only into Max this time. I laugh and grab Max's unopened beer from his hand. He doesn't fight it. "I'll let you know." I wink.

"Go get her, girlfriend," Lou encourages, thankful to see my poise blossoming again.

Lou watched me drown out much of the last eight weeks in whiskey and Alli and a three-night fling with a girl named Sam that I met in Tony's basement bar on a Monday afternoon.

There was a single line from Mabel's letter that kept ringing on repeat: "as sure of myself as you are."

Bizarre! Sure of myself? Not at all. I was sure of nothing.

And so the whiskey.

And the women.

This past Monday, Lou made the executive decision that I had been mourning Mabel long enough. She stomped into my bedroom, ripped the covers off my bed, and shouted, "Your coping mechanisms are pathetic, Emma. You need to get your shit together. If that includes therapy, I will help you find someone, but this laying around all day and drinking all night is gross and you won't be doing it anymore."

I was kind of enjoying the self-pity and was planning on riding it out until the season started, but Lou's frightening commands were well-intentioned, so I decided to muster up the energy to shower and grab a coffee and head to the library for some overdue studying.

I'm on the mend and ready to mingle on this Friday evening.

I approach Kate. She's in a conversation with two others, her teammates. I know both of them: Erika and Dani. I met Erika during freshman year in Bio 101. I introduced her to Jeremy, one of Lou's River Rat buddies, and they have been dating ever since.

Dani and I have a slightly different "friendship." We met at Kurt Dow's Halloween party sophomore year. We were both dressed up as boxers, sporting nearly identical red, white, and blue high-waisted striped shorts, navy sports bras, and taped wrists. Classic, simple, lesbian costume, but in our drunken state, we found our matching attire to be exaggeratedly ironic. The two of us teamed up for a game of beer pong and upon our victory, it seemed right, at the time, to make out rather than high-five.

Alcohol.

Dani took me back to her dorm room that night, and sometime in the early morning hours, her extremely conservative roommate walked in on us. Dani's roommate was a local and was supposed to be at a church camping retreat in Harpers Ferry for the evening. She must have decided not to spend the night in a tent because in she walked and, with a shove from Dani, off I went. Dani yanked the covers up to her chin in genuine fear. I stood naked, bedside, frozen. Her roommate shook her head in sadness, disappointment, and quietly shut the door upon her exit.

Dani later found out that her roommate had no qualms at all with the same-sex encounter. "God loves everyone, silly," she said. "But you shouldn't be having sex before marriage. I think it's best for me to move back home and commute, but if you ever want to attend my church, it's only twenty minutes away. I think you'd like it."

Dani and I haven't even shaken hands since that night, but I make sure to torment her about the terribly awkward incident every time I see her.

"Dani!" I shout as I shuffle my way into their closed circle. "Are you heading to church on Sunday?"

Dani rolls her eyes.

"Hey, Emma." Erika reaches in for a hug. "How have you been?"

"Good. And happy to see that one of you is excited to see me." I look back to Dani and wink before redirecting my attention to Erika. "How have you and Jere been?" I ask her.

She answers, but I find my attention drawing toward Kate. I smile softly at her as Erika rambles on. Kate reciprocates with a soft bend of her plush pink lips. Both of us hold eye contact, and I'm finding it difficult to break from her spellbinding stare.

"Double fisting, Emma?"

I blink, breaking my gaze to address Dani.

I remember the two beers I'm holding and immediately offer Kate the one I had taken from Max. "Need one?" I ask, handing it to Kate. I had watched her take her last sip while standing with Max and Lou and knew she needed a refill.

She gleefully accepts.

Erika and Dani instantly start giggling. Now knowing well my intention of joining their circle, they disperse, leaving me alone with Kate.

"It's Emma, right?"

An instant buzz shimmies up my back in excitement. "How do you..."

"You were in the library last week. Monday, was it?"

I nod in confirmation.

"I thought so. I was with Dani. I asked her about you."

You asked about me? "Well, Dani isn't the best person to share my finer traits."

She shakes her head as if to tell me that she knows all about Kurt Dow's Halloween party.

* * *

Kate and I pour oversized bowls of Raisin Nut Bran cereal and sit on my kitchen floor. It's two in the morning and the table is eleven feet too far for such a drunken state.

We're sitting crossed-legged, our cereal bowls between us. She leans in close enough that I can feel her boozy breath as she speaks. "You know," she says with a smile. "I've been thinking about kissing you since I saw you in the library."

"No, you haven't."

She sits back, strands of her wavy blond hair covering her face. "I have." Another spoonful muddles her slurred words. "That's a little weird, huh?"

I look at Kate, and, for a brief moment, I think of Mabel. I see her face, her freckles, her lips. I replay our first kiss at the base of my apartment steps and the Friday evening that we stood in this kitchen and ate hunks of the warm challah bread in between kisses. I inhale deeply, removing the memories from the present moment.

"Very weird," I reply. I put down my cereal bowl, grab Kate's face with both of my hands, and kiss her raisin-full mouth, hard. She places her bowl beside mine, pushes me down to the kitchen floor, and crawls on top of me as she swallows her cereal.

I do not think about Mabel another time the entire night.

DECEMBER

Saturday, December 27

"When does Kate get back?" Lou asks.

The conclusion of midterm madness sent Kate, and most other students, home for a jolly long hiatus from school and stress. Lou and I have been stuck all winter break with the rest of our teammates eating leftover cafeteria food and spending entirely too much time in the gym.

"Tomorrow evening. Not soon enough. I miss her. Can't wait to see her."

"I still can't believe you got her," Max says, holding up his hand for a high-five. I chuckle, slapping his hand away. "Same."

I really am. I'm completely surprised. Beyond her beauty, Kate is funny, like really, really, ab-aching funny. She's witty and she's smart and she's an incredible athlete and I think she really likes me.

"You two haven't spent a second apart since you met," Lou says. "I'm sure she's missing you too. Did she have a nice Christmas?"

"It sounded like it. She was all excited about some new designer handbag that her mom got her." I chuckle, finding our differences in material desires humorous.

"Fancy!" Lou exclaims.

Max chimes in. "Not as fancy as the dance moves I'm about to pull out, ladiesss!"

Lou slides into a parking spot just across the street from Pine Social Bar & Bands. A lucky find in Washington, DC. Since Christmas fell on a Thursday, Coach gave us all weekend off. A small glimpse of freedom from the daily grind. Lou and I have all intentions of soaking in every minute of it.

* * *

"Hello, pretty lady," Mabel says, handing me a clear fizzy mixed drink with a lime propped up on the rim. My heart sinks deep in my chest.

I haven't spoken to Mabel once. Not a phone call, not a text message, no emails have been exchanged. I have no idea if she came home over Thanksgiving because she never called. I never sent her the Sweet Shoppe recipes she had asked for. Complete silence for four months. I've hardly thought about her since meeting Kate, but here she is, dressed in blue jeans and red lipstick. Her hair is even longer than I remember, her eyes just as riveting.

I take the drink, knowing instinctively that I need to mimic her unflustered appearance. "This isn't roofied, is it?"

She chuckles and I take a sip.

"I was hoping you'd be here when Lou said she was coming."

I spy Lou across the bar spinning aimlessly on the dance floor and curse her silently for not mentioning the colossal fact that Mabel was going to be in Washington, DC, on this night, in this neighborhood, at this bar.

Mabel must sense my confusion because she hastily sparks up another topic. "Have you seen this band before? They're apparently a great nineties' band."

I take a deep breath, settling my emotions, forcing out the memories of our last encounter—the river mist, the canoe, her truck.

"How have you been, Mae?"

She lets out a sigh of relief, now knowing that small talk won't be necessary. "I've been okay, Emma June. How about you?"

"I've been okay too. Let's drink."

We clink our glasses together and we drink. We drink entirely too much. Sipping down vodka waters and singing along to every single hit nineties song. Each drink brings us closer, her hands on my thigh, my arm around her waist.

Then the band plays "Mr. Jones."

She grabs my hand in hers as if I am hers to hold. My heart jolts. I think about Kate for the first time all night. I think about how our hands don't fit as perfectly together as mine and Mabel's, but how she is still warm, and protective, and loving. I think about how the last two months have been wonderfully exciting and new and full of hope, and how Kate is probably lying in her childhood bedroom four hundred miles away waiting for a phone call that I'm not going to make.

I squeeze Mabel's hand tight, forcing Kate from my thoughts as we head to the dance floor. It feels natural, our bodies against each other, our eyes locked. Neon lights color us red, then orange, then pink. My whole body is heating up, goose bumps line my arms. I want to tell her I miss her. I want her. She leans in, gently grazing her lips over mine as she whispers, "I've missed you, Emma June."

I bite my lip, desperate to resist her, but she presses her warm mouth against mine and I don't hesitate to kiss her back with all of me, tasting her, remembering us, our summer.

"I've made a mistake, Em," she whispers while discreetly sliding her hand up my shirt, her lips still pressed against mine. "I've thought about you every single day since I left."

A mistake?

I feel my emotions shift from ecstasy to confusion. Confusion to frustration. She's drunk. These are drunk thoughts.

I remove her hand from under my shirt.

She would have called if she cared. She would have called if she missed me. This is stupid, I'm so stupid. I'm dating Kate.

"You're drunk," I claim, sadness in my tone as I distance myself slightly.

She tugs on my shirt. "A little." I pull away, pushing her hand aside before heading back toward the bar. She follows. "Em, what's wrong?"

The magnitude of the moment combined with the alcohol explodes within me. "I'm seeing someone, you know?"

Mabel's face sobers instantly. "I…I didn't know." She looks confused, taken aback. "I'm…I'm so sorry, Emma. I didn't…"

"You hadn't considered that? Had you? That I could be seeing someone else? We haven't spoken in four months, Mabel. Four months! And now you tell me that you've made a mistake?" I don't give her time to respond. "You know what?" I say in my drunken slur. "I made the mistake. Not you. I shouldn't have let this happen tonight. I'm sorry." I leave the bar without a goodbye.

Sunday, December 28

"I'm such an idiot," I say as I push open Lou's bedroom door, still wearing the same clothes I was in last night.

"Yes, you are," she says unapologetically. She lifts her comforter, welcoming me into her bed.

"You're gross," Lou snarks, "for not changing or showering last night."

"You're gross for letting me get in your bed," I rebut.

"Truth."

"Thanks for driving home," I say, settling in beside her.

"I didn't. Max did."

"Oh." I vaguely remember frantically texting Lou and Max from the parking lot, begging them to leave. I suppose it worked, though everything is still awfully hazy.

"Where is Max?" I ask.

"He went to the gym."

"Oh, did I call Kate last night?"

"She called you. Max picked up and told her you were a belligerent wreck. Luckily, she is amazing and thought that was funny."

I sigh, overwhelmed with my actions. "Did she mention when she was coming back today?"

"No, but you should call her and ask after you tell me what's going on with you and Mabel."

"Why didn't you tell me she was going to be there?" I ask aggressively.

Lou backfires in a similar tone. "Because you're dating Kate! I didn't think it would matter."

"Ugh, well it doesn't matter. Nothing happened."

She knows I'm lying, but a God-sent knock at the apartment door saves us from continuing our uncomfortable banter. Lou answers and in walks Kate with four coffees and four breakfast sandwiches.

"Hi, babe!" she says, her cool rosy cheeks beaming of soberness and vigor.

I smile with all the strength I can gather and welcome her into Lou's bed beside me. She kisses my cheeks over and over, saying, "I missed you so much." I can't help but to giggle at her energy.

"Did you even sleep last night?" I ask. I can't do the math well in my hungover stupor, but she must have left her parents at two a.m. to get back so early.

"I was excited." She smiles wide.

I'm a terrible human.

"I brought you guys food!" Kate grins, lifting up the paper bag. "I got one for Max too, but I guess he's not here, huh?"

"That was really sweet, Kate," Lou says. "I'll save it for him. He just went to the gym."

The three of us, tucked under Lou's coral quilt, eat the sandwiches while Lou recaps the night for Kate without a single mention of Mabel. I can't speak. My head is spinning. I haven't even showered or brushed my teeth. Mabel is still on my breath. I cringe at my actions. I hate myself for it.

Kate and I wallow back into my room. I jump in the shower and scrub intensely, hoping to remove my scandal. I crawl into bed defeated, but I'm not sure Kate notices. I think she assumes I'm just severely hungover, which is half the truth. She holds me through the afternoon as we binge-watch *Grey's Anatomy*

DVDs. I feel guilty, but her arms feel safe, and I selfishly don't want to ruin this. It's well after dark before the pounding in my head withers away and I finally muster up the decency to ask Kate how her last night at home was.

"I told my mom about you," she blurts out, as if she has been holding it in all day.

"You did?" My pounding headache swiftly returns. She told her mom about me while I was dancing with another woman. Not just another woman. My summer fling. A woman I think I loved. Love still? No. No.

I turn my body to face her, attempting to remain calm.

"I tried to call you last night to tell you all about it," Kate says. "That's why I left so early this morning. Needed to get out of there."

"Gosh, I'm so sorry I wasn't there for you," I say, genuinely wishing I could take back my actions last night. Wishing I wouldn't have had so many drinks. Wishing I would have just stayed home. "Are you okay? How did she respond?"

"I'm fine. I showed her a picture of you. Her response was, 'well, at least she's pretty.'" Kate chuckles a bit at the recollection of her mother's ignorant, judgmental, but slightly humorous response. "I would have preferred her to say, 'at least you're happy'…you know…something along those lines, but she's not wrong, you are pretty, and I guess that's better than her not saying anything at all." Kate grins, a sad grin, but a grin.

"Thank God she approves," I utter sarcastically.

From what I've gathered, Kate's mom, Faith, is the type of person that makes her children dress in their Sunday finest at the dinner table. Faith bought Kate her first Coach purse on her seventh birthday. She makes them go to tea on Sundays instead of gathering around the TV for football, and she has absolutely no problem at all with gay people, unless it is her children that are gay.

"She's so cold. I don't know if she'll ever come around fully and my dad…I don't think he cares, but he just doesn't say much at all." There is sadness in Kate's tone. "How about your dad, Em? What does he say about us?"

When I told my dad about Kate, his first response was, "Oh jeez, what happened to Mabel? I really liked her." I think he instantly regretted that when I responded, "I did too, but she left for school." He didn't say another word about Mabel and followed up with, "I'm sure Kate's even better, honey. I can't wait to meet her."

"If I'm happy, he's happy," I tell Kate.

"Are you happy?"

I stare into Kate's sappy blue eyes. She checks off every box I could want in a partner. She's kind and she's reliable. She's beautiful and driven and athletic and smart.

"I'm happy," I tell her, thoughts of Mabel creeping in. I quickly shut them down. I know that love is more than a grocery store checklist, but Kate is perfect. And Mabel is not the one for me. Kate and I are just getting started. I am happy. We are happy. Kate is surely the perfect match for me.

2009

Friday, February 20

It's early, just after five a.m., when Kate's alarm roars. The sun hasn't even cracked an eyelid. She carelessly shoves the alarm clock into the bedside table wall, knocking Mabel's white-framed picture from its flimsy pushpin to the floor.

As it crashes, I feel an unexpected worry bubble up within me and I curse Kate silently for her clumsiness.

"Shit." Kate flicks on the table lamp before reaching for the frame. "It didn't break," she says as she examines the two whimsical women closely for what appears to be the first time. "This is a really cool piece. Where'd you get it?"

"I, uh…a friend drew it."

"What friend?" Kate inquires as she shoves the pushpin back into the wall and rehangs the picture.

"Mabel. She doesn't live here anymore. I just like the picture."

Saying "Mabel" so casually makes me nervous, as if I've done something wrong.

"I like it too." Kate kisses my forehead and hops out of bed. I sigh in relief, thankful that she doesn't care to know more about this old Mabel friend of mine.

"Where are you going?" I ask.

"Early practice, babe. I told you that."

"Right." I sigh, pretty certain she never told me that.

"We're actually down on the C&O Canal today," she says. "We're running a 5k. Can I borrow a pair of socks?"

"Yes," I reply, for the third time this week. "Of course." Organization isn't her strong suit.

"It's gonna be freezing," I say, rubbing the tired from my eyes. "And really dark."

"Warmer than it's been in weeks actually: forty-four degrees and Coach has headlamps. I'm borrowing this hat too," she says, holding up my navy women's basketball beanie.

"Don't lose it."

"I won't." She winks.

She will.

She kisses my cheek and hurries out the door without turning the bedside table lamp back off. Not that it matters; I'm wide awake. I have to be at the gym in an hour for weightlifting, and even if I didn't, the very thought of the C&O Canal brings me back to a morning with Mabel so many months ago.

It was early August. 2008.

Mabel had this brilliant idea to hike the first leg of the C&O Canal: Great Falls, Virginia to Georgetown, DC.

"A few down-and-backs on the basketball court is my running limit," I told her.

"Oh, come on!" she begged. "We'll walk it. It'll be a breeze."

That was really all the convincing I needed. I was far too infatuated to say no to her.

About ten miles into the thirteen-mile stretch, I insisted we stop to rest. My legs were stiff and heavy. Mabel knew it, so she didn't bother encouraging me onward. We sat upon a massive flat rock perched above the Potomac River, and we took turns sipping lukewarm water from her CamelBak as the river rippled by beneath us.

While tracing my finger over the heart-shaped carvings others had left in the stone, Mabel slipped out a pocketknife from her bag.

"Want to leave a message?" she asked, handing me the knife.

After a moment of wonder, I etched a wobbly circle with lines shooting out of it.

"Here," I said, handing the knife back to her. "Why don't you sign our names?"

Her eyebrows raised. "Is that a sun?"

"Is it that bad?" I laughed. "You're the artist. You should have done it."

"No, no, I see it." She smiled. "It's obviously a sun. For our summer, huh?"

"Exactly. The best summer."

I snap out of the memory, log on to Facebook, and type in Mabel Ann.

She's changed her profile picture since the last time I scrolled over her page. I suppose that's not too surprising; it's been months since I've consciously sought out her whereabouts.

In her newest photo, she's wearing a gray hoodie with UNCW stamped across her chest in bold turquoise lettering. There's a fishing pole propped up beside her. I recognize the pier in the background. She's in Southport. She's holding a decent-sized mackerel in her perfect freckled hands and her seaweed eyes are thrilled.

I wonder if her brother took this picture.

I wonder if she's happy, if she thinks of me. If she thought I would see this picture.

I wouldn't dare ask.

MARCH

Saturday, March 7

Regardless of the outcome of our championship game, our coaches determined it would be best to stay in a hotel afterward to digest the season as a team. Being the only two seniors, Lou and I secretly packed two bottles of bubbly each, certain we'd be popping it open with our team after a victorious final buzzer.

We were heartbreakingly wrong.

We lost by seven, fouling them in the final seconds only to drift further and further from victory.

Lou and I couldn't bear the sight of the hopeful underclassmen that still had another year or more of opportunity, so we took our booze and locked ourselves away in our hotel room for the night.

"It all goes so fast," Lou says, reaching for her half-empty bottle on the bedside table. Our room and my nose are so stuffy I can hardly breathe.

Five hours ago, I had consciously tucked in my jersey. I had laced my shoes tighter than normal, and I had pulled up my hair into an impeccably neat ponytail. I took in every bit of that freshly painted wooden floor, the bright lights overhead, the crowd swarming in to cheer us on, my dad sitting three seats up from half-court.

"So fast," I repeat, my eyes still swelling with tears.

Every bone-chilling morning spent hurrying into the locker room before sunrise, every weight I lifted, every shuffle, sprint, and slide. All of it is rushing through me. "We had a good run, though."

"A good career," Lou adds.

I huff, falling hard into my bed, appreciating the dimly lit hotel room for echoing our melancholy moods so well.

I scroll through my messages, rereading what Kate wrote: *Hell of a game. I thought that three you hit from the baseline with 3 minutes left was gonna change the tide. Oh well, we can't all be conference champs ;). KIDDING. You played great. Sending big, big HUGS to you and Lou!*

Kate's only a junior. Her soccer squad won the conference this year and I know she was trying to make light of my career-ending situation, but in my depressed state of mind, I would have preferred a simple, *I love you.*

I scroll past messages from my Uncle Joey, my grandparents, and another from my dad before eagerly blurting out, "Mabel texted me."

She had texted me moments after the game ended, but I knew Lou would give me a hard time about it, so I waited until we had enough alcohol in our system to help buffer our responses.

Lou's eyes light up. "Why?"

I lift my phone and read the message aloud. "You played great, Em. What a wonderful career you've had. You should be proud of yourself. Sending love to you and Lou."

"She must have watched the game online?" Lou slurs. "Did you know she was following our season?"

"I didn't." I had no idea. Absolutely no idea, and though I should have found it strange, I didn't. I found it sweet. Flattering even.

"My God. You two. Do you guys talk frequently?"

"No! Never."

"Well, are you going to respond?"

"Should I?"

"Yes, of course. We've already lost the game, why not lose Kate as well?"

I delete the message to satisfy Lou, but thoughts of Mabel have already fogged my clarity. I find myself entranced by the pale moonlight streaming in through the crack in the thick burgundy drapes.

What's the harm in writing back?

Why do I even want to write back?

Why am I thinking so obsessively about her stupid text?

Fuck.

When Lou eventually drifts off to sleep, I write Mabel a hundred different messages before settling on, *Thanks, Mae.*

When the morning creeps in through the gap in the drapes, I hastily reach for my phone, hoping Mabel has responded with some way to extend our conversation, but there's nothing, and I'm disappointed in myself for feeling sad about it.

MAY

Saturday, May 23

"Surprise!"

I pulled up to Louie's work thinking that Lou, Max, Kate, and I were taking an evening rafting trip down the Potomac. I was very wrong.

Kate sprints up from the crowd and wraps her arms around me as I hop out of my car looking dumbfounded. "Umm…this is for me?" I ask, taking note of the of the large "Congratulations on Graduating, Emma!" banner hanging above the kayak rack and the many pods of navy and gold balloons scattered around the patio.

"I know you're not a huge fan of the whole surprise party thing, but I was talking to your dad and Lou about it a few months back and I just really wanted to do something special for you."

She steps back, trying to decipher my reaction.

I look astonished. I know I do and it's because Kate knows I don't like surprises and it's also because she knows I was looking forward to a peaceful stroll down the river. Still, this over-the-top gesture should not come as a surprise at all. Kate adores all things over-the-top. Overpriced ridiculous heels, trendy gold foil facials, rich chocolates, and she loves to give. Gift-giving is her love language. Small gifts, typically, but in this case, a surprise graduation party for twenty-five.

I shake off my ungratefulness and look around at the many people I love. My grandparents, my dad, Louie and Max, teammates, a few other friends, and, of course, Kate. Her genuine smile warms my distaste and I relax, soaking in the lovely moment.

"Thank you so much, babe," I say. "This is so, so thoughtful."

Friends cycle through to squeeze me one by one. Many of them also graduated this morning and were thrilled to take advantage of the free beer. When Louie finally budges her way in, she nudges me and says, "I knew you'd be pissed, but Kate was persistent and look how sweet she looks over there?" We chuckle as we watch her shotgun a Natural Light beer with my grandfather.

My dad follows Lou's hug and comments similarly, "I know this isn't your thing, but it's nice isn't it?"

I nod, agreeing. "It is nice, Dad. Thanks for helping to pull it together."

"Louie really pulled through with the venue and Kate did all the legwork. I pretty much just brought the booze."

I tilt my head in gratitude. "And I see you got Billie to come BBQ?"

I've known Billie my whole life. He's a high school friend of my dad's. He has a food truck business and Dad hires him for any and all events. Big or small.

"Of course I did. He's serving up his best for my girl." Dad winks and pulls me in for a big bear hug.

I indulge in Kate's savory chocolate chip brownies, a boatload of Dad's finest beers, and Billie's famous BBQ.

"You would have preferred the river, wouldn't you?" Lou asks, interrupting my stare. I was watching Kate line up a fourth round of flip cup, admiring her level of energy from across the patio.

"No, no." I chuckle. "This is great. Thank you again for helping with it. Kate really is so thoughtful. Isn't she?"

"You don't have to convince me." Louie grins, nudging my arm.

The party dwindles down around ten thirty, leaving my dad, Kate, Lou, Max, and me to clean up the odds and ends. I give Kate a hug to thank her again for the generous gesture I never wanted.

She hugs me hard and says, "I knew you'd like this better than a stroll down the river. We can do that any day."

"Yeah, you're right," I say, trying to recall the last time we spent any time at all on the river. It's been a while. A really long while.

Journal: Monday, May 25, 2009

I don't want surprises.

I want normal. Boring.

I want to drink coffee to jazz music. Write a little. Work a little. Laugh a little. Make some love. Binge some TV. Go for a jog as the sun goes down. Sip soup and sleep well.

I want simple.

There is something so simple missing.

Tuesday, May 26

"Congratulations!" Kate shouts as I walk into the Blue Moon Diner.

I hush her from the front door with a wide-eyed grin. "How do you even know if I got the job?" I question as I settle into the rickety wooden chair across from her.

"Oh, please," Kate says. "I know you got the job. You're glowing."

I flip my hair back and grin. "It must be the lighting in here."

My dad's longtime law buddy, Ray, retired from his firm at fifty and kicked off Pulse Eagle, a Mid-Atlantic beer distributor. Since Ray opened the company two years ago, he's been asking me to come work for him as a sales rep.

He'd say, "You have the competitive edge, Em. And the personality."

I called him up the morning after graduation and today he hired me, as promised, to help him branch into bars, restaurants, concert halls, stadiums—basically anywhere that can handle a tap.

"Well, are you gonna tell me if you officially got the job?" Kate asks.

"I officially got the job." I wink. "Say hello to the newest regional sales representative."

I feel proud. Since basketball ended, I've been eager to find a new competitive passion and I think Pulse Eagle can offer that.

"Well, hello, Miss Regional Sales Rep." Kate smiles wide as she hands me an oversized gift bag.

"What is this?" I whine as I tilt my head in confusion. "I told you to stop spending your money on me!"

Kate spent last summer and most of her winter break working at a family friend's vineyard in upstate New York. According to her, they pay exceptionally well and the boozy clientele tips generously. They must. Unless her parents are supplementing her fruitful lifestyle. I've never asked, though. Her money is her business. I just wish she wouldn't spend it on me.

"Oh, stop it," Kate insists. "It's just a little something."

"A little something? You just threw me a graduation party."

She waves off my response. "Go on, open it."

I force a smile as I unravel a perfect bow and remove the neatly packed tissue paper. It's evident that she took pride in wrapping this. It makes me feel special.

I lift a chestnut leather work tote from the gift bag. I'm in pure disbelief. Despite the overkill of surprises from Kate, this gift is so incredibly thoughtful. It's sophisticated and stylish and is exactly what I need to kick off my professional career.

"The graduation party and now this?" I grab her bright blue eyes with mine. "It's really beautiful, Kate. Perfect. Really perfect. You didn't have to do this."

She flutters her long eyelashes and flips her silky blond hair behind her shoulders. "Oh, I know. But I wanted to."

"I love it," I confirm, letting the moment soak in.

Here I am with this beautiful, generous woman, sharing conversation and a meal on a Tuesday afternoon. What more could I want?

JUNE

Thursday, June 12

Max is in the midst of a summer-long internship with the Frederick Keys, the single-A affiliate to the Baltimore Orioles. Lou, Kate, and I have become regular attendees to the Frederick stadium. Lou and I love a good baseball game and Kate loves cheering for Ketchup to beat Relish and Mustard around the bases during innings.

We all love the five-dollar beers.

Tonight is an especially exhilarating night. With Max's assistance, I got a meeting with the Nymeo Stadium Concessions Manager, and tonight, they are featuring a five-dollar Batter's Bait IPA from one of my clients Bait Brewery out of Brunswick.

This is my first legitimate deal, and Lou, Kate, and I plan to skew the sales numbers for the evening by celebrating with however many beers we can fit into nine innings.

"Yes!" Kate shouts much too energetically as the condiments line up on the big screen over left field. We're standing on the upper deck right next to the beer tent. I want to be able to see what beers the fans are ordering and urge every passerby to check out the new IPA on draft.

"I'll go grab us another round while Kate cheers on her beloved Ketchup." Lou chuckles, rolling her eyes.

Unfortunately for Kate, Relish is rounding third for a sure victory when I feel a tug at my arm.

"Emma. Hi."

I spin around, knowing well her voice. "Mabel."

My heart floods with joy at the sight of her sweet freckly face. I reach in for a timid hug, breathing in her smell, still familiar.

It has been just over a year since we first met at Pickle's Pub by Camden Yards. Ten months since she drove away from my apartment. Six months since I last felt her lips against mine.

"You're back in town?" Realizing this is a dumb question, I follow up with, "Obviously."

"Just for a few days," she confirms, her eyes steady on mine. "I'm moving back down to North Carolina."

"To read more and fish more, huh?" I say, repeating what she told me a summer ago at the Pickle's Pub bar.

Her cheeks brighten, perhaps flattered that I recalled our conversation. "I'm actually moving to Durham." She nods. "I got in to law school. At Duke."

"Law school? Wow. Congratulations. I...I didn't know that was something you had actually decided to move forward with."

My thoughts swirl. Why would I know? We haven't spoken in months.

"Yeah," Mabel says. "Actually, it was your dad that really sold me on pursuing it." She pauses for my reaction, but I'm speechless, nodding at her with a forced smile. She continues, "How has life been for you?"

The word "life" shoots me back to reality, to my life. I quickly reach for Kate's hand, embarrassed I didn't introduce her sooner. "This is my, my Kate," I stutter.

"Girlfriend," Kate corrects with a smirk, reaching for Mabel's hand. "Nice to meet you."

I find Kate's subtle confidence comforting and stabilizing.

"Girlfriend." I smile, squeezing Kate's hand in assurance.

"So, do you have a place down there yet?" I ask Mabel, eager to move past my fumbling introduction.

"I do," Mabel says. "Just a Craigslist find. Random roommates."

"That's great. Exciting."

"It is. Thank you." She smiles genuinely before waving over Jack.

"We're not..." she stutters. "Together. We're just..."

I cut her off as Jack nears. "Hey, Jack." My throat is in the bottom of my gut. He gives a head nod and I wonder if his half-assed hello means he knows that I slept with Mabel days after they broke up last summer.

"Well, it was great to see you, Mae. And you, Jack." I can hardly make eye contact with either of them. The discomfort is sweating off me.

Kate grabs my hand firmly and says, "Nice to meet you both," before assertively leading us down the concrete bleacher steps.

"Did you date her or something?" Kate asks as we settle into the seats that we had zero intention of sitting in.

"Kind of." I shrug, doing a poor job of hiding my emotions. "Just for a summer."

"What summer?" she probes, wrapping her arm around my shoulder.

"Last summer," I say, flustered and angry at myself for feeling like I have to hold back the tears swelling in my eyes.

"Last summer? Is this the same Mabel that drew that picture you have hanging above your nightstand?"

I inhale deeply, gathering every bit of my sanity before grabbing Kate's hand that's hanging over my shoulder. "Yeah, but it was nothing really, just a summer thing. Don't even think you could really call it dating."

"Interesting...Kinda surprised you've never mentioned her to me. Looks like she switched teams anyway, huh?"

"Guess so." I force out a chuckle, desperate for Lou to sweep in and save me from myself. On cue, she hurries in with our refills.

"Here you go, ladies!"

Lou passes the beers to us, settles in beside me, and discreetly rubs my arm as if to say she saw Mabel and Jack and she knows what I'm feeling right now. She must sense a little tension, so she pipes up. "Sorry about Ketchup's loss today, Kate."

"It was close!" Kate chuckles, gulping down her beer.

* * *

Kate runs out to get the car, so I can catch up with Max to thank him again for helping me close my first sale. The moment she scurries away, Lou throws her arm over my shoulder and whispers, "You doin' okay?"

"I'm fine," I tell her as we walk toward the stadium offices. "I mean what are the odds?"

"Well..." Lou hesitates. "Actually, not terrible, since we go to almost every game and she really likes baseball and this is the only stadium in town."

I elbow Lou.

"You still love her, don't you?" Lou asks, already knowing the answer.

"I don't love her. I'm with Kate."

"So, you're with Kate and you love Mabel."

I give Lou a dirty glare. "Enough, please. I really don't want to talk about it."

I feel Lou's eye roll pierce through my lies.

* * *

It's nearly midnight. I have a slight headache. Stress-induced. Maybe a little alcohol-induced too.

"You want to talk about seeing Mabel at the game?" Kate muses carefully.

We're in bed, I turn over to face her, our bodies parallel now. "Not really."

"You're sad about her?" she says, tucking my loose hair behind my ear. "Did she hurt you?"

"No, no. It was just weird seeing her."

"You haven't seen her since last summer?"

My thoughts race back to December. Mabel's warm, drunken lips against mine at the neon-lit bar in DC. I cringe inside at my irresponsible actions. I cringe because I've thought about Mabel's lips too many times since Kate and I have been together.

I lie. "Yeah, a year ago."

"It's always hard to see people you once loved."

"I didn't love her," I firmly state, attempting to convince both Kate and me that this was and is the truth.

Kate doesn't flinch, and I appreciate her nonjudgmental, genuine conversation.

"Well," Kate says. "It's always hard to see people you once liked, then."

"Yeah, I guess so." I grab Kate's face and kiss her gently. "You're perfect."

Friday, June 13

It's 10:00 a.m. and I haven't gotten out of bed yet. Kate left for the gym an hour ago. I told her I was too tired to join. I am tired, mentally exhausted. I can't decipher my feelings about seeing Mabel and I'm not quite ready to shove the thought of her behind me again.

My cell phone buzzes beneath my pillow. It's Mabel. Impeccable timing.

Hey Emma, I hope you don't mind me reaching out. I just felt the need to tell you that Jack and I aren't a thing. I know you probably don't even care, but I just couldn't let you think that I'd gone back to him after last summer. The two of us were just catching up.

My tears revel up. Another message buzzes through.

You look happy, Em. Kate is beautiful and she's so very lucky to have you.

I delete both text messages and crumble into my journal.

Journal: Friday, June 13, 2009

She's like reading a paperback book in a hot bath. Beads of water staining the character I've fallen madly for, reminding me that she's not real beyond these pages.

But still, I think of her, and I imagine up the rest of my very real life with her.

The simplicity of it all.

She's painting, braless, asking me if the fruits in the garden are ready for picking, and I don't crave anything more than the moment she hands me a ripe blackberry and tells me, "Wait until you try this, Emma June." I'll take a bite and her whole face will light up and she'll ask me, "This is the good stuff, huh?"

"The best stuff," I'll tell her, and she'll know I'm not talking about the blackberry.

"Looks like you need this," Kate says, pounding in through the bedroom door with a Lost Dog to-go coffee cup. My favorite coffee in town. An endearing gesture. The kind that tugs our relationship along.

I slam my journal shut and reach for the cup appreciatively.

"Writing?"

"Nothing worth sharing."

"Well, I'm glad to see you writing. I haven't seen you in that journal in some time."

I've had nothing to say, but I don't tell her that.

She yanks off her sweaty clothes, leaves them in the middle of the floor, and hops in the shower, chatting with me over the running water about her workout and an email she got from her soccer coach about their new trainer.

"Where is he from?" I speak loudly, but, per usual, when she tries to converse with me while she's in the shower, she can't hear me over the running water.

"What?" she shouts. I don't feel like screaming, so I don't respond at all. A moment passes and she shouts again, "Can you come in here to talk to me? I can't hear you." I don't respond again. It seems like too much work to roll out of bed at this young hour on a Friday. She knows I'm ignoring her and still lying in bed, so she shouts once more. "You want to go to Betty's for breakfast?"

I hear the water shut off and watch her as she fills the doorframe, wrapped in a towel, still dripping wet. She's gorgeous, but I'm not sure why she can't dry off in the shower. I watch a puddle form onto the bathroom tile as she asks again, "What do you think? About breakfast?"

I lift the bedsheet and motion for her to come get back into our bed. She drops her towel at the bathroom door and crawls in beside me. Her bare skin, damp against my fingertips, smells of lavender. She undresses me piece by piece with the midmorning sun streaming in through the cracked window blinds. I let her. I want to love her.

* * *

"Do you ever think of our future?" Kate says. Our bodies exhausted, sticky, side by side.

"What do you mean?"

"You know, next year at this time, I'll be done with school. We don't have to stay here. We could move to New York City or DC. Even Los Angeles if we want."

"I dunno. I like it here," I tell her.

"I do too, but don't you want something more?"

Maybe we both do. "I don't think so. I'm not sure, actually. I'm just settling into this new job. Why don't we just wait and see what happens?"

My phone rings, giving me an easy out from the conversation.

"It's Lou. Let me grab this. She wanted advice on a work situation."

Another lie.

I answer and tell Lou to hang on just a moment. I roll out of bed, where Kate and I have been laying the morning away and head out of the bedroom into the kitchen.

"Can you talk?" Lou asks.

"What's up?" I say quietly, knowing exactly why she's calling.

"I just want to say something about Mabel. Kate can't hear right?"

"Go ahead," I urge. I only picked up because I know Lou and I know she would continue to call and bother me until she says what she needs to say.

"You still love Mabel, and you should do something about it."

"No. I don't. She was with Jack last night!" My voice is quiet, but straining. It's very clear my emotions are running wild.

"Who cares if she was with him?" Lou interjects.

"I don't. I don't care. I'm with Kate. We'll talk later." I hang up without a goodbye.

SEPTEMBER

Wednesday, September 9

"Look at this." Louie tosses two bags of Counter Culture coffee beans on the kitchen table and shoves an already-opened envelope into my hands. She's winded, as if she's just sprinted up the stairs to deliver this message.

"I like your nails," I tell her as I unfold the envelope. "Interesting choice of colors."

Her shirt is splattered with mud from a day's work on the river, but her nails are painted an impeccable denim blue.

"I know, love this color, it's called Canoe Blue. Fitting, right?"

"It is."

"Okay, now read!" she demands, pointing to the letter.

"Okay, okay."

Hey Louie, this is a little strange, but I know Em is seeing Kate and I didn't want to cause any confusion, so I thought I'd just send these to you at work and you can pass a bag along to Emma.

Counter Culture started in Durham. The first organic roaster in the whole state and the best coffee I've ever had. I know you and Em appreciate a good mild roast, so I wanted to share. Hope you and Max are well. Send Emma my love.
  -Mabel

I look up from the letter at Lou, feeling baffled by the gesture.

"What do you think?" Lou asks, her eyes wider than usual.

"I...I have no idea what to think."

"Well, it's thoughtful, right?"

"Or is it just inappropriate? She knows I'm with Kate. It's weird if Kate even finds out she sent this."

"Well, then don't let her find out." Lou tosses her hands in the air as if she's shocked at my reaction.

I don't shake my look of confusion.

"Oh, come on," she says. "She sent it to me, not you, for that reason, so at least she thought it through."

"I really don't understand why she sent this? And she said, 'send my *love*'? We haven't spoken since the Keys Game back in June. *Love*. Really?"

Lou scratches her head and looks as if she's going to say something but instead rolls open the bag, grinds the beans, and starts a pot of coffee.

After a long stretch of quiet, Louie chimes in. "She was thinking of you. And I know you've thought of her too."

I close my eyes for a moment and let out a big sigh before responding. "I have thought of her, yes, but I'm actually in a really good place right now with Kate."

"Listen, I'll say one more thing about this, then I'll leave you to it, but I know you like Kate. I like her too. She's wonderful. But I also know that you have unresolved feelings for Mabel. This was her olive branch. You decide what you wanna do with it."

Lou hands me a steaming cup and sits beside me at the table.

"Have you thanked her yet?" I ask before we both take a small sip.

"Not yet."

"Can you let her know I was very appreciative?"

Lou looks up from her coffee with an empathetic smile. "Of course. Now what's your thoughts? I taste nutty. Sweet. Smooth."

"It's really good," I tell her. "Simple."

OCTOBER

Saturday, October 24

"Lou, no." I stomp my foot. "We're not going out."

"Oh, you bores," Lou groans. "Max and I will be the life of the bar without you, then."

"Well, that wouldn't change even if we were there." I grin.

Lou smirks, satisfied with my backhanded compliment.

"Have fun!" we bellow as Lou slams the door behind her and Max, leaving Kate and me to enjoy the apartment alone for the evening.

We're celebrating our one-year anniversary, and I've been begging Kate for weeks to not plan anything at all. I told her, "I just want to be at home. With you. With pie. No surprises. Please, nothing."

Last Saturday she surprised me with a red rose and an Italian dinner date. She insisted that it had absolutely nothing to do with our anniversary.

"You've been working hard, and I just wanted to treat you," she claimed.

She cannot help herself and I had been craving chicken parmigiana, so I embraced the unnecessary treat.

"Just the two of us, finally," I say while pouring steaming spiked cider into two mugs. "I got you a little something."

"You made me promise there would be no presents!" Kate whines.

"I made you promise not to get *me* anything. You've done enough. And this is just a silly thing anyway." I head into my bedroom closet and return with a key-chain tracker. "It's for your keys." I smile. "You just download an app on your phone. So now, every time you lose your keys, you can click the panic button on the app and an alarm will sound. No more lost keys."

She laughs. "You know me so well."

"Now we just need to find your keys to hook it up," I say, scanning the living room.

"We can do that tomorrow," Kate insists. "Come sit next to me."

I toss Kate a burgundy knit blanket and cut two pieces of pumpkin pie before curling up on the couch next to her. The classic Halloween flick *Hocus Pocus* plays as we snuggle in close together, chomping away on our dessert.

At commercial break, Kate looks at me, puts down her cider and her pie, and presses her hand against my cheek.

"Oh no, babe," I moan, my hands still full of the treats. "Please tell me there are no surprises."

She chuckles. "No, no surprises. I just…I love you, Emma."

One whole year has passed by and we have yet to tell each other, "I love you." I've thought about saying it when we've showered together and she kisses the back of my shoulders. When she flashes a syrupy smile at me over a pint of ice cream. When she asks about how my day went and engages in the details.

I've thought about it a hundred different times and I've never said it and I've wondered why she hasn't said it to me, but as I fall into her deep blue eyes, I know she means it.I place my mug and pie on the coffee table beside hers and take her hands, squeezing them tightly without breaking eye contact.

I think about how much I love this. How much I love this perfect autumn evening with this kind, wavy-haired, perfect woman, and before my silence becomes concerning, I reply, "I love you too."

She grabs my lips with hers. "I've been wanting to say that to you for months, Em."

"What have you been waiting for?" I ask.

"You to say it first."

"I was waiting on you!" I snap back with a laugh.

She straightens up her posture and grabs my hands. "I've been hesitant because sometimes you just seem distant. Tough to read. I know you have a lot going on with work, so it's okay. All good." A smile erupts across her face, exposing her pearly whites. She wraps her long arms around me and pulls me in. "I love you and I wanted you to know that."

I fall into her, nuzzling my face into the side of her neck, inhaling her presence, wondering if the words I've just spoken resonate in my soul or if I've just told her that I love her because it is easier than saying, "You are perfect, by all standards, and I think I might love you too. But I'm not sure if it's just the thought of us that I love."

I'm just not sure.

DECEMBER

Friday, December 4

"It just seems silly for us to spend this much on rent when we have no idea how our finances are going to play out over the next year."

Kate tilts her head and begs me with her best puppy dog eyes.

It is a nice spot. It's an open, airy loft just around the corner from my beloved Sweet Shoppe, in the heart of downtown Shepherdstown. Not far from where Lou and I have been living. I'd like to stay where I am, but Lou is leaving our humble abode for a Harpers Ferry cabin with Max.

It's frankly overdue. In fact, I'm certain Lou has only waited this long to move in with Max to allow me time to settle into my new job, finances, and feel out my relationship with Kate a bit longer. It sounds slightly pathetic now that I think about it, but nonetheless, appreciated.

So, here I am house-hunting with Kate.

When I don't budge at her puppy eyes, Kate speaks up. "Please, Emma, it's perfect! The lease is month to month, if we can't make it work, we'll move out. But why not?"

"Why not? Because we can live two miles down the street for half the price."

"And it's half as nice," she cries. "Come on! We're getting boring. You know it and I know it. We need change."

I offer her a smile because she isn't wrong. We are getting boring. The one-year mark hit, we exchanged "I love yous," and now I was left wondering if our relationship had run its course. I assume, based on her "boring" comment, that she's feeling the same.

My smile was clearly more than Kate expected because she stretches her grin from ear to ear and continues her pursuit of convincing. "Listen, remember when we were considering DC? Isn't this better?"

I nod in agreement. I am thankful DC was dropped. Kate had nearly persuaded me but ended up accepting the grad-assistant position with the women's soccer team, so we were here to stay. For now, anyway.

"You love this town. And we'll be walking distance to all the restaurants and the river."

I sigh, too exhausted from holiday work hours to argue anymore. "All right. All right. What the hell. Let's do it. Let's move in."

"Thank you!" she cries, pouncing on me for a tight hug. "The holidays are going to be perfect this year. The Christmas tree will look so nice by the fireplace, and we can set up your candlelight thingy in the front window."

"It's called a menorah, Kate. A menorah."

Wednesday, December 9

"Are you going to leave it behind?" Lou asks as she plops down beside me.

I'm sitting cross-legged on my wooden bedroom floor holding the watercolor painting from Mabel in my hands. Other than the overgrown pothos vine, my final duffel of clothing, and this picture, the room is empty.

"I don't want to." I feel like I'm leaving a part of me behind in this apartment. College, Lou, every memory with Mabel. I didn't expect to feel so sentimental about this pretty typical life advancement.

"Take it with you, then." Lou smiles without judgment.

"Have you spoken to Mabel at all?" I ask, knowing the two catch up periodically.

"I did, actually," Lou replies. "It was about a month ago now. She said law school isn't as miserable as she thought it would be. She's seeing someone now. A girl."

"Really? You know anything about her?" I ask, still staring at the colorful pencil figures in the picture frame.

"Her name is Naomi. Apparently, she's half Indian, so on top of her beautiful skin, she has an amazing wardrobe of traditional garb that she pulls out for big events. She's a year ahead of Mabel in law school…said she's super smart. She seems good overall. Happy."

"Guess Mabel finally came out to her family?"

"She did." Lou nods. "In her words, 'they were amazing.'"

"Good."

"She asked about you, ya know?" My eyes perk up, curious to know what she said. "Just asked how you were doing, if you were still seeing Kate."

I nod, acknowledging what Lou has said but unsure how to feel about it. We sit quietly together, soaking in the last moments in the apartment that we have shared so many special moments in. She can tell I'm struggling with the transition, and she knows if it weren't for her moving in with Max, I wouldn't be moving in with Kate.

I try to reassure her that I'm ready for the move. "I'm excited to move in with Kate." I look up from the picture at Lou. I think I mean it. A fresh start sounds nice. The thought of waking up next to Kate to enjoy a slow morning, to just be, it all sounds nice. "I mean, we're over a year into this, but I just kinda feel like I'm going through the motions right now."

Lou doesn't say anything, just nods to let me know she's listening. I'm not expecting her to say anything. I'm just venting. I inhale then exhale, my breath extra loud in this empty room.

"I do love her. I do," I continue. "And so I should probably leave this picture behind, huh?" I chuckle, understanding the silliness of this silly small piece of artwork and the silly fact that I'm sitting in an empty room contemplating this silly thing.

Lou takes the frame from my hand and tucks it neatly into my duffel.

"You can get rid of it another day. Come on, let's go get a drink to celebrate the end of this epic era."

Wednesday, December 23

"This is where you live?" I ask, bewildered.

Kate and I pull in through a brick entryway that opens to a gigantic, smart-looking, brick home with a dark slate roof and tall white columns dressed in twinkly Christmas bulbs. Each window wears a red bow wreath, and lush garland is draped neatly around the front porch railing.

On cue, her mom and dad exit the oversized wooden double doors to greet us, and I'm now the leading actress in Hallmark's newest Christmas film.

"Home sweet home!" Kate winks, waving at her parents through the front windshield as she parks.

I sling my leather duffel over my shoulder and grab my hostess gift: a Christmas Cactus, planted in a hefty white clay pot.

"Hi, Mrs. Miller." I offer my friendliest fake smile, praying it appears genuine as I hand her the blooming plant. I'm a bit nervous. I've overheard one too many gossipy conversations between Kate and her mother, and Kate has spilled at least a dozen lengthy rants about this woman. This, in combination with her mother's blatant distaste for Kate's sexuality, has left me uneasy about spending three whole nights here.

"Thank you," Faith replies, eyeing the cactus keenly from all angles before reaching out her cold, thin hand to firmly shake mine. "It was this time last year that Kate informed us about you." I offer a sheepish smile, unsure of how to respond. She continues, "I understand you've been missing out on Christmas your whole life?" Her quirky thin head tilts to the side, awaiting my response to what I think is a joke.

"Yeah, I, uh…" I chuckle awkwardly. "I guess so."

I glance over at Kate for help, but she's in a big bear hug from her dad.

Faith continues, "Well we're happy you could join us. Here, let me show you to your room." I'm not sure this invitation is genuine, but I follow.

The inside of the house is as grand as the outside. Dark hardwood floors dressed in plush runners, sky-high ceilings, endless natural light. Faith sprint-walks up a steep, windy, garland-wrapped staircase, down a short hallway, and into the guest room. I'm not sure of the rush, but I lug my bag in close stride.

"You'll stay here," she directs. "Make yourself at home." I thank her, but I'm not sure she hears it. The door shuts sharply before I can even spin back around.

* * *

I'm splashing water on my face when Kate barges in.

"You didn't tell me we were sleeping in separate rooms, Kate," I whisper, careful not to let Faith hear my complaints.

The moment the words leave my mouth, I regret them. I shouldn't complain. I know bringing me home was a stressful decision for Kate, and I promise myself to be less whiny and more supportive through the remainder of the trip.

"I knew you wouldn't want to come." Kate chuckles and brings me into her to kiss my forehead. "It's only a couple of days. You'll be okay, right?"

I smile at her and take note of the wood-framed king bed and the beautiful snowy landscape lying outside the large bedroom windows. Mrs. Miller had even added a red-and-green-checkered throw pillow to accompany the warm seasonal decor that floods the rest of the house. "It is a nice room. I'll be fine."

She leans in and presses her warm lips against mine. She moans softly, slipping her tongue in unexpectedly. It makes me wish we were in our room in our own apartment, free to undress. She removes herself with a smirk, knowing I've enjoyed her tease.

"Come on," she says. "Get ready, will ya? My friends are waiting for us. You're going to love them."

* * *

"I just don't like them, Lou."

"Well, with that attitude, I can't imagine they like you much either."

It's one thirty in the morning. I didn't actually think Lou would answer, but I'm thankful she did. I need to vent.

"I'm serious, Lou. If you met them, you'd feel the same. It's like I don't even know her with them. First of all, they were dressed in fur coats and black dresses. We were at a fucking bar. A shitty bar. I had Converse tennis shoes on! And I don't need your judgey comments, I was dressed like a normal human would dress when going to a shitty, shitty bar. I mean, Kate could have at least warned me to spruce up a bit. I felt out of place."

I don't give Lou any time to comment on my judgments, or on my completely predictable choice of shoes.

"And you know not one of them asked me a single question. They didn't care to know a single thing about the girl their friend is dating. And also, one of her friends made fun of some stranger's jeans, and another one of them was talking about how it's not going to work out with her current boyfriend because he is too poor. It felt like fucking middle school. Shallow beyond belief! And Kate even laughed. She was laughing at it all. I couldn't believe it. She's like a mean girl."

"Okay, okay, deep breaths," Lou says, sensing my panic. "That doesn't sound like Kate at all. She hasn't seen her friends in a while, and she's never brought a girl home. Why don't you just give her a break?" I can hear the tired in Lou's voice. She is over my ranting and I'm getting tired of hearing myself complain as well, but I need to get a few more things off my chest, so I continue, "I don't even feel like I'm important to her. She basically ignored me the whole night. I knew I shouldn't have come."

"Listen, Em. Go to sleep. I promise you will wake up with a different outlook tomorrow. You know Kate. She will come around. This is a lot for her. Give her a little credit. I'm sure she is trying to maneuver through all kinds of emotions right now. I will check in tomorrow, all right?"

"Fine. You're right. You're right. Tell Max I said hello and Merry Christmas. Thanks for picking up."

Thursday, December 24: Christmas Eve

"Lou told you to call, didn't she?"

"No, no. I'm just checking in on my girl."

"You're a terrible liar, Dad." The sun is creeping in through the frosted windowpane. The clock on the nightstand reads 8:15 a.m. I rub the tired from my eyes. "But, I'm doing okay."

He doesn't feel the need to acknowledge the fact that I called him a liar. "Are Kate's parents nice?"

"They seem fine. Kate and I went out last night, so I haven't spent much time with them."

"Did you like Kate's friends?"

"They were fine."

"Hmm." He wants me to expand, because he's already gotten the lowdown from Lou and knows I have more to say.

"It sounds weird, but ya know, when we're home, in Shepherdstown, we're in this little bubble of familiarity. It's our town. We have our little home, and our friends. It's our space, and now we're in her space, and I just don't really feel welcome in her space."

"Well…" He hesitates. "Do they have good booze you can drink to get you through the next two days?"

His timely humor brings a smile across my tired face.

"I'm being ridiculous," I continue. "I guess I just didn't really want to come in the first place based on the things Kate has shared with me about her family, and I need to just suck it up and change my attitude."

"Hon, it's okay to feel the way you're feeling. Hell, I don't think I'd want to hang out with those parents of hers either after hearing what you've told me. But Kate is a good person, and she gets that from somewhere. Try to be positive and supportive for her. At least for the next two days. Okay?"

"You're right," I assure him. "I will be."

"Well, I'm running out for a bike ride. Do you guys have plans today?"

"We're apparently going to tea." I know my dad can hear the lack of excitement in my tone, so I try to spruce up as I close out the conversation. "I'm sure it'll be a great day."

"It will be, Em. I love you."

"Have a good ride. I love you."

* * *

The brisk upstate New York air cuts through my wool parka, biting at my skin. Kate's parents, her brother, Ryan, Kate, and I are awaiting our table for tea. I suppose these people are used to this kind of cold, but my teeth are chattering and my fingertips are numb. I step toward Kate, hoping to nuzzle up next to her, but the hostess calls for the "party of five Millers" and she hastily brushes me off. God forbid we stand too close to each other.

The four of them walk uniformly through the mossy front doors and I stagger behind, annoyed with their militant behavior. I feel like their family pet. Following suit. Staying quiet.

"You know, Emma, Kate's always been a superstar." I sip on my tea and smile and nod like a good dog does. Mrs. Miller hasn't stopped talking since we sat down. Her sunken cheeks and squeaky voice resemble a mouse, and I can't stop envisioning her as one.

"She played varsity tennis," Mrs. Miller boasts. "Varsity basketball, and soccer too. And my favorite moment, of course, was watching her and her boyfriend, Chris, walk down that homecoming court." Her eyes waver off to the left as if she's reliving some magical moment.

"Mom! He was not my boyfriend," Kate corrects, glancing at my straight face. "And we were on the court. We didn't even win. I was literally dating Julia and you guys didn't know."

Her mom huffs, annoyed with Kate for tainting her wonderful imaginary memory.

"That's enough, Mom," Ryan chimes in. "We're over hearing about Kate. I wanna hear about me now." Ryan is older. He's in the School of Medicine at the University of Buffalo. He and Kate don't talk much when they're apart, and I haven't seen them chat at all since being together, but I appreciate his self-centered save at this moment.

"Well, Ryan," Mrs. Miller begins. I doze off into an imaginary world where I'm in my bed, eating processed foods and binging Harry Potter movies. Alone. My not-so-subtle daydreaming is starkly interrupted when it's time to leave.

"Emma!" Kate shoves me, nearly knocking me from my chair. "You okay?" She knows I haven't heard a thing and her grimace pours disappointment. "Let's go."

I hurry up from my padded chair and follow her out.

Saturday, December 26

A text comes in from my dad, *You on your way back?*
Yes, I write back.
He responds, *Praise Jesus!* I can't help but to chuckle at his hilarious response.
"What's funny?" Kate asks.
I know this tone. She is about to unload on me.
"Nothing," I reply.
"Nothing? You haven't laughed since we crossed the border into New York on Wednesday, and now we're on our way home and you're not only laughing, you're more involved with whomever you're texting than you were with a single conversation over Christmas."
"Whoa, it's just my dad. Calm down. Why are you so frustrated?"
She doesn't need to answer. I know why she is frustrated. Yesterday, after a cinnamon-roll breakfast that we needed to shower and "dress appropriately" for, the lovely Faith had started talking about my job as a sales rep.

"You don't aspire for anything more?" she asked.

"I'm not sure. Maybe one day, but I like it for now."

"You seem very smart. A shame to waste that, don't you think?"

I stayed stern, refusing to smile or waver from my stubborn stance. "I don't think I'm wasting anything. I like my job, and I'm good at it."

Mrs. Miller persisted, and I felt my short temper bubble up within me. "I'm sure you are," she said.

Kate chimed in to silence her mother. "Em, you were talking about possibly branching into other areas in the industry." She nodded her head, urging me to expand on my aspirations so that her mother's disappointment would subside. "Right?" Kate nodded again, essentially begging me to cooperate. "Why don't you share?"

I've talked to Kate at length about my desire to one day own and operate my own brewery, but these are my aspirations, my dreams, and my goals to share as I please, and I'm certainly not going to fabricate some far-off dream to appease this mousy woman. I shook my head, refusing to do as Kate wished. "No, I'm quite happy where I am." I smiled a bitchy smile.

This altercation led to a very silent Christmas afternoon, and dinner, and evening, and morning, and now very long car ride back to Shepherdstown, West Virginia.

Kate inhales deeply. "You didn't even try this weekend."

"What do you mean?" I respond entirely too loudly. "I shouldn't have to try at all. I was myself and that clearly isn't good enough for you or your family."

"Silent Night" perks up on the radio, and we appropriately don't speak a single word for the remainder of the car ride.

2010

FEBRUARY

Thursday, February 18

"I have a launch tomorrow at the Bavarian Inn, any interest in coming?"

It's 7:45 a.m. I'm curling my hair for the workday. I just started this whole curling of the hair thing, and Lou says it's "very adult" of me. I agree with her. I've also started using eye shadow and ordering guacamole on my burrito bowls. I've come a long way.

"Mmm, tempting," Kate says. She's lacing up her tennis shoes for a quick workout before her ten o'clock class.

"Why do you have to put your shoes on in the house?" I ask for the third time this week.

Kate ignores me. "What's the launch going to consist of?"

"Like every other launch." My tone is harsh, so I pause briefly to gather enough kindness to perk up. "We're going to start sourcing all of their beers, so we're offering free tastings for the guests. You know, the usual. You don't have to come. It's just a happy hour thing."

The Bavarian Inn is a European-inspired boutique perched high above the Potomac River. It's a Shepherdstown staple known for its exclusivity and charm. It would be hard for Kate to pass up an opportunity to snoop around the premises, but we haven't been the same since Christmas.

We weren't ever going to be the same again.

We were in good graces by New Year's kiss, but the trip back to Kate's hometown exposed us. We're different. We don't want the same things. We don't value the same things. And above all, we just don't have the kind of love that can overcome family quarrels—or hometown glitches. We don't have the kind of love that's made for the long haul.

Instead of tackling our relationship issues head-on, we've let it mull over, driving us into this stale, unbearable routine of complacency.

Wake, work, sleep.

Wake, work, sleep.

We're drifting apart. Yet neither of us have mustered up the energy, or concern, or courage to have a meaningful conversation, or plan a date, or, God forbid, have sex. We've just accepted this lost love, and we're carrying on a whole lot like roommates.

Distant, complacent roommates.

"Yeah, I'll pass."

Whew.

"And hey, Saturday, I'm gonna go into DC with Becca and Sandra. Is that all right? We didn't have plans, right?"

I take a deep breath, pondering how we got here and why we're still pretending like this. "Yeah, that's fine."

"Cool." She hops up from the bed and heads to walk out the door, but hastily stops. "Hey, ya know, I wasn't gonna say anything, but I..." She walks back toward the bathroom door to make eye contact with me. I'm still curling my hair. "I can't seem to shake it. I saw the picture in the hall closet. Ya know, the one Mabel gave you?"

Sweat boils up on the back of my spine as I try desperately to appear unshaken. "I totally forgot about that picture," I tell her, not looking away from my reflection in the mirror. It's the truth. I did forget about it. I moved it in with me two months ago and buried it deep in the hall closet and haven't thought about it since.

"You coulda hung it up if ya liked it. I just think it's weird that you left it in the closet. Like you're hiding it."

I put down the curling iron and face her. We're an arm's length apart and I've never felt farther. "It is weird." I nod my head in agreement. "It's weird, and I'm sorry that it made you feel uncomfortable."

Her pistol-blue eyes squint. I can't tell if she is angry or frustrated or confused. "Okay," she says as she shakes her head and shrugs her shoulders simultaneously. "Okay then."

She leaves.

APRIL

Journal: Monday, April 5, 2010

We settled in. Safe and sound when I needed that.
Thought I needed that.
Thought I needed stable. Reliable. Comfortable.
But I'm uncomfortable;
tiptoeing around what I've convinced myself is this sane, logical partner.
Convinced myself that she is the only choice.
She's a good choice. A great choice. Just not the choice for me.

Friday, April 9

"You two go do your baseball thing." Kate beams as if she'd bought the ticket herself as a present for Lou.

"Thank you, thank you," Lou cries, smashing her face all over Kate's cheek.

Ray had given me two free tickets to Opening Day at Camden Yards as an appreciation gift for my first year with the company.

We demolished all expectations. We coordinated local charity fundraisers and we were a part of multiple restaurant launches and community gatherings. We picked up thirteen new clients, tapped into thirty-plus bars. Got into a handful of new venues and expanded our trucking services to keep up with the pace.

The progress of it all has been equal parts infatuating and exhausting. Kate receives the brunt of it. Every week that passes, we grow more distant from each other. It feels both sad and natural. We still have conversations in the evening and she still wraps her long arms around my willing body as we sleep, but it's clear we're just treading around the inevitable end.

Wake, work, sleep. Wake, work, sleep.

I initially thought the baseball game might be an opportunity to reconnect a bit, though I'm not sure what good it would do. It didn't matter anyway, because when I asked her she alleged she was in over her head with schoolwork and grad-assistant duties, which I'm sure is true.

Frankly, I didn't mind. Lou has always been a better baseball companion anyway.

* * *

"Soooo..." Lou says hesitantly while she drives us down Route 70 toward Baltimore. "Did you see that Mabel might be downtown today?"

"Where would I see that?" I ask, counting the months in my head that have passed since I last spoke to Mabel. Ten. It's been ten months.

"On Facebook or Twitter. You know, anywhere in the twenty-first century."

"I must have missed it." I silenced her profile nearly a year ago, so I would only be alerted of her doings if I purposely searched for her name.

"What is she here for?"

"She's doing some event for our people."

"Our people, huh?" I roll my eyes.

"Yes!" Lou laughs.

Lou likes to group herself into the LGBTQ community because she claims she is always gay. "Get it?" she always says. "Happy!" To which I always confirm, "There's space for everyone."

"Well," I say. "What is it that she's doing? Details, please."

"I saw it on Facebook," Lou begins. "I'm not quite sure, but I think she's a member of some group called the Love Rules Foundation. They promote upcoming propositions and fight against social injustices. Pretty sure they're walking around the stadium today passing out pamphlets and bracelets and stuff."

"Cool," I say, feeling anything but cool on the inside. I'm amazed at myself for still feeling shaken by just the sound of her name.

"Cool indeed. Especially the bracelets. They're tie-dye and they say, 'Love will Rule.'"

"Very cool," I say again.

I feel anxious as I let the power of Mabel's name encroach upon my mood. She is doing something that matters—exactly what she said she was going to do. She must be so happy, and I have this innate desire to hear all about it.

"She really made a one-eighty with the whole coming out thing, huh?" Lou says. "She's always posting about LGBTQ issues and propositions, and it appears she is still with that Naomi chick."

"Sounds like she's happy," I say, pretending not to care, but I do care. Because very few people knew about Mabel and me. Not like people know about Mabel and Naomi. She must be proud of Naomi, proud of herself. Their relationship together. Mabel and I were just a secret. Hers to share, but one she chose to keep.

* * *

I wish Lou hadn't said a word about Mabel. I can't stop thinking about her. I'm distracted and uninterested in drinking or cheering.

Does she love Naomi?

Is she happy?

Does she ever think about me?

I'm struggling to enjoy the afternoon. When Lou and I walk into Pickle's Pub, I think I see Mabel leaning against the bar standing right where we stood on the first day we met, but it's not her. I think I see her walking to the restroom, and then again standing at the front door of the bar, but it's not her. Of course it's not her. This city is massive. The chances of running into each other are slim to none.

Lou and I finally make our way into the stadium, and I know once we walk through the gates, my chances of miraculously running into Mabel diminish. I'm pathetically devastated by it. By the seventh inning, I'm so antsy that I tear Lou from the bar and beg her to head out early. She knows instantly there is no arguing my request.

"What's going on?"

"I think I have to break up with Kate."

"Why? No, you don't. Well, actually," she stutters a bit, letting my conviction soak in. "Perhaps it is time to do that." I see Lou bite her lip and I know she is wondering if she did the right thing by expressing her approval on this matter.

I exhale heavily. "Kate and I have been hanging on by a thread for months. It's clear as day. I know you know that."

Lou nods in agreement. "You two just don't seem happy. You deserve to be happy." Lou reaches over and grabs my right hand, cupping it between both of hers.

"You're thinking about Mabel." Lou knows, and she shakes her head. "I shouldn't have mentioned her name earlier. I just thought you should be prepared in case she showed up. That was stupid, but what is it about her that always gets you so worked up?" Lou's tone is sympathetic, almost worried. "It's been a lifetime since you've spent any significant time with her. You don't even know her anymore."

She's right. I don't know Mabel anymore. She doesn't know me. I made Lou leave opening day because I am sulking over a stranger that I spent three months with nearly two years ago.

"I don't know what is wrong with me." I sigh.

"Well, try to explain," Lou says. "Please."

I don't think she's angry we're leaving. It's been a long afternoon, and she's probably excited to go home and order Chinese food with Max.

"I just wish I had never met her." I take a deep breath, trying to settle my whirlwind of emotions. "When I look back on that summer, it seems…perfect. Every single day of it. I just can't shake her. Or the idea of her, I guess. I'm crazy, aren't I?" I carry on, not giving Lou the opportunity to respond. "Kate and I don't have that spark. Maybe we did at first, but there's just something missing. I think maybe there has always been something missing."

Lou inhales deeply, trying to absorb my scattered rambling. "Emma," she says, cautiously. "What you had with Mabel really was wonderful and you know how I feel about potentially exploring that avenue again, but what you have with Kate is great too. I want you to think everything through. You're not in college anymore. You have a real career now and responsibilities and Kate has been there for you through all of these amazing life changes."

I think about the last year and a half I've spent with Kate. She cheered me on as I walked across the stage to receive my diploma and she was by my side when I landed my first real job with Ray. She doesn't like baseball and she doesn't care for art or nature the way Mabel did, but we talk about important things, things Mabel and I never talked about: our stresses, our worries, politics. I think about Kate's *Saturday Night Live* obsessions and how she adores puppies and spaghetti and how she cries when she sees old people. I love her beauty. As vain as it sounds, I love to show her off. It feels good to stand beside her. It feels good to date the former soccer star, the newest Graduate Assistant. It feels good to have someone.

"I care for Kate. I do. She's not the one, though, Lou. I know it. I've known it."

"That's good. It's great actually!" Lou exclaims. "You and Kate have created amazing memories together over the last year and a half, but I'm glad you're figuring things out. You know what's best for you. If this is the end, then it's time to end it."

"I need to end it."

Sunday, April 11

"Hey, Kate, do you have a minute to talk?"

Kate shuffles in from the living room and sits down at the barstool against the kitchen island. She pulls her phone from the pocket of her sweatpants and starts scrolling almost immediately. Her actions are symbolic of our relationship. Here, but not really here.

"What's up?" she says, not looking up from her phone.

I'm standing opposite her. I inhale deeply as I glance around our living room, the home we've grown apart in for the last four months. Our wobbly floor lamp sways back and forth, casting swing-dancing shadows against the pale walls. I plop my elbows against the granite countertop.

"Listen," I say. My urgent sincerity must spark Kate's interest because she instantly sets down her phone to refocus her attention.

"I don't know how to handle this, but things have…they've changed between us." I have been rehearsing this conversation in my head repeatedly since Friday, but I choke on each word as it leaves my lips. "I…I know you feel it too."

Kate nods in agreement, tears promptly swelling her eyes. "This is it for us, huh?"

My eyes swell too. The knot in my throat growing painful as I nod.

I tell Kate that I'll sleep on the couch, but she offers to head to her friend Becca's for the evening. "We can figure out our game plan in the morning," she says. I've already investigated our lease and know that it requires a two-month notice, so we'll be juggling this separation dance until, at least, June.

Kate spends a few moments stuffing odds and ends into a backpack. She takes my navy Shepherd University hoodie. I don't say a word, though I know it's the last time I'll see it. I don't mind.

She stands at the door and takes a moment to look around the room. She's not crying. Neither of us are. "I'll see you tomorrow," she says with a dull smile, then leaves.

She's relieved. I am too.

Monday, April 12

"I want to open a brewery."

"You broke up with Kate, didn't you?"

I pause for a moment. "How did you know that?"

I hear Dad sip his coffee on the other end of the phone. It's 6:45 a.m. I imagine he's sitting on the living room couch. He's dressed for work—slacks and a tie—his feet propped up on the glass coffee table, the *Alexandria Gazette* draped over his thighs.

"There's a little pep in your voice that I haven't heard in a while."

What the fuck? "Thanks for your sympathy."

"I'm not too good with these things, huh?"

"No, Dad. You're not."

I hear him shuffle around. Probably removing the newspaper from his lap and straightening up his posture to try and rebound from his abrasive remark. "Your mother...she would know just what to say. But listen, I knew you'd eventually figure it out. Kate was a great girl, but she wasn't the one, Em. Tell me how you're doing though. You're feeling all right?"

I exhale deeply. He means well and he's right. She's not the one.

"I'm good. Relieved, actually. Anyway, can we talk about the brewery?"

"Sure. What can I do?"

"Well, I need some more training, some real experience, and not from you, Dad." I hear him groan. Although I've learned all I know from his garage brewing adventures, I need something more to really feel comfortable moving forward. "I was thinking about calling up Uncle Joey and seeing if he had some space for me on his team."

"I think it's good timing. You know I was just talking to him this past weekend. Apparently, he's growing like crazy. You should absolutely go for it. I bet he'd be thrilled to have you on the team."

"I'm gonna do it."

"You should. I think it will be good to get outta town for a while too. Live somewhere new. What better place than the mountains of North Carolina?"

"I was thinking the same."

"Have you told Ray? He's gonna be crushed, huh?"

"Ehh, I've been talking about branching out for a while now. I don't think he'll be too surprised."

"All right, well, make sure you tell him sooner than later."

"I will, Dad."

"I know you will. Proud of you, kid. And hey, Em…"

"Yeah, Dad?"

"When you're ready to open up your own brewery, I'm here to help you get it up and running, but will ya come on home? Relocating the law firm would be a real pain in the ass."

"I can do that. Love you, Dad."

MAY

Sunday, May 23

"We need to do this more often," Lou wheezes. "I might not make it up this thing."

Kate chuckles, barely winded. "Oh, come on now, Lou. We're almost there."

Lou has absolutely no idea that Max is waiting at the peak of the Maryland Heights trail waiting to propose to her. Kate and I were tasked with getting her to the top, which was easy, as Louie's always down for an outdoor adventure.

"Guys, I'm going to sprint this last leg," Kate says on cue. I wave her on gleefully, knowing she is only hustling up ahead to find the perfect camera angle before Louie and I round the bend.

"Overachiever!" Lou huffs. The moment Kate takes off, Lou is in full gossip mode. "Why in the hell are we hiking with her? I mean I love her, but you lesbians are so weird."

Kate and I haven't spent much time at all together. I'm certain she is already hooking up with someone new because she's constantly on her phone, rarely comes home, and when she does, it's long after I've fallen asleep. We haven't shared a bed. She has claimed the couch and swears it's more comfortable than our "old sunken bed." When we're both in the apartment, we small talk and occasionally we'll even enjoy a morning coffee. Frankly, we're so busy with work that our extremely unusual living arrangement hasn't even fazed us.

"It's not that weird," I assure Lou. "We're friends." It is weird, but this is a two-person job, and Max knew he could rely on Kate and me to get it done regardless of our current relationship status. I need Lou to believe me, so I continue, "I mean sure, our living situation is…different. But it's temporary."

Lou rolls her eyes. "Still weird. I guess it's not much longer though, huh? Gonna miss you, ya know."

"We can cry together later, Louie." I slyly fall back behind Lou, careful not to intrude on her magical moment as we round the bend to the overlook.

"Max?" Lou says, confused. She looks back at me, then glares at Kate, searching for an explanation from either of us. We both smile, and she looks back toward her college sweetheart.

"Come on over here, Louie," Max says as he gets down on one knee, his arms stretched toward her.

Kate and I can't hear what Max tells Lou from where we are standing, but we watch as he holds the rest of his life in his palms and we cry when he wipes the tears from her face and we snap pictures of him sliding his grandmother's gold-banded diamond ring onto her finger and we cheer loudly when she finally looks back at us and shouts, "We're gettin' hitched!"

* * *

"That was beautiful today wasn't it?" Kate says, sliding off her windbreaker and socks.

We both came back to the apartment tonight. I haven't seen Kate on her phone all afternoon. I assume she doesn't have any plans.

"It was perfect," I reply.

Kate hops onto the bed. She hasn't slept here in over a month. She waves me in and I comply, allowing her to wrap her right arm and leg tightly around my body. It's been two months since we've laid together and it should be weird, but it's not. Not at all. Like we're so far removed from what we used to be that even the awkwardness is behind us.

"You want to get married one day, Em?" Kate talks like we're old friends.

I hold her body close to mine, knowing she's not referring to her and I getting married, but just asking out of curiosity.

"Yes, I'd like that."

"Me too. Maybe at a vineyard. Somewhere in upstate New York by my family. You know, there are talks of New York legalizing gay marriage soon?"

"I sure hope they do."

"Me too," she agrees. "I want a big wedding. All the people I love. Everyone. An amazing band. In May, or maybe April. What about you?"

"I think I'd like something small," I tell her. "Just close family. In a backyard maybe. Somewhere with a whole lot of big trees and draped lights. Some sunflowers. September would be nice. Maybe October."

Kate kisses my cheek and says, "That sounds really beautiful, Em."

In this moment of pure difference, I feel at peace. She stays in the bed, and we sleep with our backs against one another, both of us knowing this will be the last time our bodies are so close. I move out, way out, in just a few days.

JUNE

Tuesday, June 1

"You *sure* you have to go?"

"Yes, I'm sure, Louie. It's not forever."

"I know! But who is going to help me decide what flowers to use in my bouquet?" she cries. "And what color should the linens be? And what about the dessert?" She sighs dramatically. "I'm being selfish, aren't I?"

Lou has been obsessively planning every detail of her and Max's September wedding, down to the yellow button mums that will greet the guests and the custom pumpkin beer I'm to make during my time in Asheville.

I nod and bring her in for a tight hug.

Lou kisses my cheek and leaves Kate and me to say our goodbyes.

"So, this is it, huh?" Kate sighs.

We're out of our lease as of yesterday. I left her all the furniture, which wasn't much, and helped her haul it into her new apartment down the street.

"This is it." I grab her hands. We look at each other for a moment and I wonder when I'll see her again. Lou and Max's wedding, probably. Will she have a plus-one? Will I?

"You're gonna be great, Em." She grins. "Can't wait for you to open that brewery one day."

I feel a pit in my stomach. Not a sad one, just nervous, and a bit overwhelmed maybe. I'm holding the hands of something that was once so wonderful and I'm going to let go of it, willingly. And I'm going to let go of my stable job, and I'm going to let go of this little town that I love so much. This whole state. I'm leaving it all behind.

I squeeze Kate's hands and kiss her cheek. "Take care, Kate."

* * *

It's two coffees, a Sheetz turkey sandwich, and four hundred miles down 81 South into Bent Creek, North Carolina.

"Welcome home," Uncle Joey says, wrapping his burly arms around me and lifting me as he did when I was just a child.

"Hi, Uncle Joey."

Uncle Joey lived a few houses down from us for much of my childhood. At the time, he worked some high-profile government gig in DC. He'd leave before dawn each morning and get home after dinner. To this day, I have no idea what he did, but I know he owned a closet full of the same boring black suits and thick red and blue ties.

The day after we buried Mom, Uncle Joey quit his job. Dad and I went over to his place for a bonfire fueled by all his black suits, his black leather briefcase, and a whole lot of wood. A month later he had sold his property in Alexandria and headed off to hike the entire Appalachian Trail solo. "It's time to start checking things off the bucket list!" he gleefully said.

Mom's death brought him back to life. The irony.

After his hike, he settled, first in a camper in Fletcher, North Carolina, and now in a small wood cabin in Bent Creek. He never could let go of the camper, though. It's been parked in the wooded area behind his brewery for the last six years.

"I just put a new window unit in the camper, should keep ya cool all summer."

"Thanks for letting me crash here, Uncle Joey."

"Of course, Emmy. Stay as long as you want. I'm looking forward to having your help at the brewery. Ya know the beer scene down here is boomin'. Got two new kettles comin' in Monday."

In 1999, Uncle Joey bought a rundown 1860s church in Bent Creek, just outside the Asheville city limits. He preserved what he could: all the stained glass, the altar, which now acts as a band stand, and a few of the pews. My dad helped refurbish the thin-planked hardwood floors, and the two of them installed concrete countertops. Joey snagged two commercial-grade copper kettles from an estate sale in Culpeper, Virginia and four more stainless steel ones, and opened up Holy Local Brewing in the summer of 2000.

"Well, I'm excited to be here and learn a few things," I tell him.

Uncle Joey smiles in the same cartoon way I remember: round rosy cheeks, beaming. "Shouldn't be long before you're running your own place. You still brewing with your dad much?"

"Every now and then."

"It's like riding a bike." He winks. "Let me show ya round."

His once straight-edged lingo has relaxed. It's hard to even picture the old Uncle Joey. The suit and tie. The buzz cut. He belongs here with his overgrown beard and his infectious smile.

"These two kettles here"—he points to the copper kettles in the far left of the brew room—"are for experimental beers. We just released a blueberry saison for this summer. Anything you can think up, we can do. We'll rotate 'em through. And these four work horses brew the staples year-round. The Bent River IPA, the Blue Ridge Lager, the Catawba River Stout, and the Kayak Sipper Pale Ale. You'll know the recipes like the back of your hand by the month's end."

I smile, reaching over for a side hug. "Gonna be a good summer, Uncle Joey."

"I've missed ya, kid."

Uncle Joey has been dating the flower-crown-wearing hippy Martha for the last seven years, but they never had kids and I've always felt like I've filled a little void for him.

"Well, go on and get settled in the camper," Uncle Joey insists. "There's a fridge full of food in there to get ya started. Martha and I have to head to that art exhibit tonight. I think I told ya about that? One of her friends from book club is the big feature."

He rolls his eyes as I nod in confirmation.

"I'll see ya in the morning. Nine a.m. sharp. We open at eleven. Sleep well."

* * *

The camper door screeches loudly as I pull it shut. The walls are wallpapered in white shiplap. Before Martha, they were a grimy yellow, but that was years ago. A decorative tin backsplash stretches behind the stove and the sticker-covered white refrigerator. There are three open wooden shelves holding four white coffee mugs, and a handful of matching white plates and bowls. A tie-dye peace sign tapestry hangs above the pull-out couch where I'll sleep, and multicolored Christmas lights line the ceiling. I crack the small window above the stove and pour a little water into each of the three snake plants that line the sill.

My phone rings. I know it's Lou. I text her and tell her I'm helping Uncle Joey in the brewery and that I'll call her later. I don't feel like talking. I wash my face, flip open my suitcase, and change into a fresh T-shirt and jeans. Before I hang the remaining clothes, I pull out the only artwork I brought with me: the watercolor painting from Mabel. Feels good to see it again. I tack it up beside my bed, unpack the rest of my life, and stuff the suitcase into the tiny closet before heading out for downtown Asheville.

I feel fearless, or just alone enough not to care about venturing out solo. It's Pride month across the country and I've already scoped out the evening's events. Crooked Women Brewing Co. is having an open mic and their Raspberry Glitter Sour Ale sounded enticing.

* * *

I park downtown, walk into the glass front door, and approach the marble bar top. A rainbow flag dangles from the ceiling. The bar is slammed with women, most wearing something colorful. I lean in and order the beer I'd already scoped out.

"It's delicious!" I hear from nearby.

I look over at the woman I've squeezed in beside. Her jawline is sharp but feminine. Her hair is shaved on the sides, a perfect wave on top and a bit reddish, which accentuates her warm, smooth skin. She is the kind of lesbian that straight girls swoon over.

"I'm excited to try it," I say, eager to make a friend.

"I'm Millie," she says as she stretches her neck around my body. "And that's my girlfriend, Jane."

Jane looks exactly as one would imagine after seeing Millie. Long blond hair, tiny frame, impeccable smile. Can't confirm, but likely never dated a woman before Millie. A magazine-worthy pair.

"Oh, I'm...I'm so sorry," I stutter, stepping back from the bar, allowing Jane and Millie to reconnect.

"Hi, Jane," I say as the bartender hands me my drink. The three of us toast "to strangers," and I'm introduced to a whole slew of their lesbian entourage, each one friendlier than the next.

"So, you quit your job, broke up with your perfectly good girlfriend, and moved to Asheville to work at your uncle's brewery?" Jane summarizes.

Hearing it aloud makes me wonder if I've made a huge mistake.

"Yes," I say.

"Well, who wants to go check out the brewery on Friday?" Millie hollers, looking around at her friends.

Everyone drunkenly high-fives before Millie confirms, "We'll be there at five on Friday."

Friday, June 25

"You return again!" Uncle Joey shouts as Millie, Jane, and the rest of the crew walk in for their fourth consecutive Friday Happy Hour.

I don't recognize one of the girls, but her bouncy hair is as rich as midnight and her deep golden complexion reminds me of a sunrise my dad and I once saw over Redfish Lake in Idaho. I'm instantly drawn to her.

Uncle Joey and I pour each of them a free taster of our newly released Mango Cream Ale, and his face lights up when six of the seven ladies follow up their taster with a pint. I nudge him and whisper, "We make a good team."

"This was all you, girl. I'm keeping you around!"

It was my idea and mostly my recipe, so I let the genuine compliment from Uncle Joey sink right on in.

Millie reaches over the bar to hug me. "Hey, Emma, this is my friend Tobin. She lives in Durham. She's visiting for the week."

"Durham?" I smile faintly, feeling the stab of Mabel against my chest. Mabel, the stranger I last saw a summer ago. In June. In Frederick. At the Keys baseball game. One whole summer ago.

"Yeah, you have friends there?" Tobin inquires.

"An old friend," I say. "You like the beer?" I ask, urgently shaking off her question.

Her eyes glitter. "It's great!"

The brewery closes at ten, and just as we have done the previous three Fridays, the girls and I head twenty yards behind the brewery and light up a bonfire just outside the camper's front door. I light the tiki torches and turn on the multicolored string lights that line the outside of the camper before sitting in the conveniently empty seat beside Tobin. I catch Millie's attention and she winks, nodding at Tobin, wanting me to confirm whether I'm into her or not.

I ignore her.

It's nearing midnight. Everyone other than the two designated drivers has had entirely too much to drink.

"Emma, how's the camper life?" Tobin asks.

"Simple." I smile. "Want to check it out?" I like showing it off. It's eccentric and very Asheville.

"Yes, I'd love that." She hops up from her Adirondack chair and heads to the camper door. I follow. Millie whistles. I hush her with my pointer finger. Thankfully everyone else seems too wrapped up in their conversations to notice Tobin and I slipping away.

We step in. The door creaks, per usual, as I shut it behind us.

"This is adorable." Tobin swirls around the room, taking note of every little detail. "You blend right in here, ya know?" she remarks as she flips through a stack of Uncle Joey's records.

I shrug my shoulders. "I'm not really sure if that's a compliment."

"It is." She winks, flopping down on the pull-out bed that I never actually pull back in. She waves me over flirtatiously with a "come, come" gesture, patting the empty space on the bed beside her. I head over as a tingling sensation scurries up my spine. The last time I felt the thrill of a woman was with Kate. So long ago now, it's hard to remember this newness, this kind of excitement.

Tobin turns on her side to face me. I do the same. "I mean, I don't know you," she says. "So, this could all be a wonderful show, but you seem relaxed. Happy. You're not the type to stress, huh?"

"I can be," I tell her.

She puts her hand on my cheek and looks at me a bit longer. Just when she is about to lean in for a kiss, I hear Jane's piercing demand. "Tobin! Let's go. We're leaving!"

"Can you stay?" I ask, flustered by urgency.

She hops out of bed, runs out of the camper door, and hurries back no more than a minute later. "Jane or Millie will come get me in the morning if you can't take me back to town."

"I can take you back," I say, relieved to have her company for the evening. It's been nearly a month since I drove away from Kate, and I miss having a warm body next to me.

Tobin turns on the radio. The same country station it's been on for, likely, the last six years starts belting and she pulls open the refrigerator.

I laugh, loving how comfortable she's made herself. I hop out of bed, butt her aside, and pull a frozen pizza out from the freezer. "Is this what you're looking for?"

"Yes." She presses her hands together in prayer and hops back on the bed to await her pizza.

"So, who's the friend you know from Durham? Another lesbian? Maybe I know her."

"Old friend," I correct. "We don't really talk anymore."

"Ah. An old love, you mean?"

I smile. "Hardly."

"So, who is she?" Tobin quizzes.

"Mabel?" I say, wondering if the name will ring a bell.

"Mabel Pickett?"

What the hell. My heart races. "You know her?"

"Yes, of course I know her. We're both lesbians in Durham."

I hesitate a moment before mumbling, "You…you know her, know her?"

"No, no!" Tobin chuckles. "I'm good friends with Karen, though."

"Karen?"

"Yeah, Karen and Mabel have been seeing each other. It's relatively new. I wouldn't call it dating, exactly. I think it's a convenience thing. They're in law school together."

"I thought she was dating some girl named Naomi?"

"So, you still love her?" Tobin's eyes widen along with her curious grin.

"No!" I rein in my defensiveness. "My friend Lou had mentioned a Naomi to me."

"Mm-hmm." Tobin rolls her eyes. "She was seeing Naomi. I think she cheated on Mabel. Can't be certain, though. I remember Karen filling me in on some former relationship of Mabel's."

I shouldn't be so overwhelmed with the news, but this small, small world is weighing on me. "Small world," I say, avoiding eye contact.

"You loved her!" Tobin cries once more.

"No, I did not," I firmly state, no longer able to hide the defensiveness. "We had a summer thing. Years ago."

"Right." Tobin's grinchy smile is wider now. "Karen and Mabel aren't really a thing. I'm telling you. It's like a space-saver situation."

"It doesn't matter, really. But you can tell her I said hi, though."

"You can tell her yourself." Tobin is thrilled to share her breaking news. "Mabel is gonna be down here in August! My friend Julie is having her bachelorette party here and I'm pretty sure Mabel got the invite because of Karen. I'll be here too. And Jane and Millie know the bride-to-be, so I'm sure they'll drag you into the festivities."

Excitement wiggles through me, my cheeks red from holding in a smile. Tobin doesn't tease me about it. She carries on for another hour over thin crust pizza and about the ins and outs of the lesbian scene in Durham.

An hour ago, I thought we were going to hook up tonight. Now she's lying beside me, her arms across her chest, red pizza sauce on her chin. She's snoring, exhausted from our gossip session. And I can't stop thinking about the possibility of seeing Mabel again.

Journal: Sunday, June 26, 2010

It was a
Lovely
Orchestrated
Vibrant
Emotion
Fluke or grand design?
The summer, the bar, the baseball game, now Asheville.
Coincidence or grand design?
Does she think about it at all like I do?

AUGUST

Thursday, August 26

"Emma!" Uncle Joey yells from the bar. "Your phone is ringin'!"

I sprint from the back office to pick it up. It's Millie. I take a deep breath to ensure that I don't sound too anxious. I've been waiting for her call all week and can't even believe I left my phone out of sight. "Hey, Millie." I speak calmly, though I feel the sweat start to bubble up on my forehead. It's a muggy Carolina morning, but it's not the heat flustering me, it's Julie's bachelorette weekend, which means Mabel will be in town, which means I desperately want to hear Millie say that they are coming into the brewery on Friday.

"Hi!" Millie says. "I know you're at work, but ya gotta sec?"

"Yeah, yeah. I was just labeling those pumpkin beers I was tellin' you about. You know, the ones for Louie's wedding?"

Lou had just asked me for a keg of "Something delicious. And pumpkin!" so I took her scant direction and delivered a light pumpkin ale with a heavy dose of spices: cinnamon, nutmeg, allspice, ginger and, of course, pumpkin. Lots and lots and lots of cans of mushy pumpkin. An easy seasonal sipper to pour all evening, but I wanted to do a little something extra as well and Uncle Joey was on board to help me get it done.

He asked one of Martha's incredibly artistic friends, Isabella, to design a nifty label in exchange for a custom twelve-pack of her choice. I emailed Isabella an engagement picture of Louie and Max, and forty-eight hours later she sent over a digital copy of the final design: a cartoon image of Louie in a white flowy gown, holding the hand of Max, who's dressed in a white button-down and jean shorts. Both are barefoot—just as they are in the picture I sent over. Yellow mums, pumpkins, and twine frame the two. Above the image is the name I chose for the beer, "The Gourdgeous Life." And below the duo is the wedding date: September 18, 2010.

My heart raced in joy when I saw the brilliant design. Better than I could have possibly envisioned. I hastily bought two hundred brown glass beer bottles and just as many labels. Enough for each guest to take one home and dozens of extras for Lou and Max to drink over the next few months as they bask in their new marital status.

The only downfall is that I hadn't calculated the time it would take to stick these custom labels around two hundred brown glass bottles. It's quite a bit of effort, but on this morning, it's a nice distraction.

"Ah!" Millie exclaims. "Yes, I remember, do we get to try the final product?"

"Actually yeah, we made enough to get us through November, most of it anyway. We'll tap it on Friday if you guys are planning on coming in?"

Please say you're coming in.

"That's why I'm calling. Of course we are coming in. You know it's Julie's bach this weekend, right?"

"Oh yeah, yeah, I remember."

Of course I remember.

"Well, if it's okay with you and Joey, could Jane and I come early tomorrow to hang some balloons up for her? I know we'd really be intruding on the space, but thought it was worth an ask?"

"Absolutely, you can. It's no problem at all. I'll talk to Uncle Joey, but I'm sure we can come up with some kind of drink special for you guys as well."

"That would be amazing. You're the best! Thank you. Thank you."

Millie's been a pleasant crutch. She and Jane. From the very first night I moved to town the two of them welcomed me into an easy friendship. Exactly what I needed. They've invited me hiking and barhopping, and to see Amos Lee play at the Orange Peel downtown. To top it off, they've become some of Holy Local's most loyal patrons. And now, I have them to thank for bringing Mabel here.

"Someone special coming in this weekend?" Uncle Joey smirks. Clearly my appearance is not as calm as I thought my conversation sounded.

I feel my face redden instantly.

"Come on! Spill, will ya?"

"All right, all right." I chuckle. "Mabel is her name. I haven't seen her in a while."

"How long?" he inquires.

"Fourteen months." I realize how pathetic I sound as it leaves my lips.

"Hmm. You counted." Uncle Joey nods as his eyes widen. "This is exciting!"

I nudge him. "Don't you say a word about it when they're here, Uncle Joey." He motions his pressed fingertips along his mouth, insinuating his lips are sealed.

"I think she might be seeing someone anyway."

"But maybe she's not." He winks.

Maybe she's not. I can't even believe how eager I am to see her. Not too long ago, I would have cringed at the idea of it. Fear, I suppose, of feeling something I shouldn't feel while dating Kate. Annoyance, maybe, that after two whole years I still feel butterflies at the very mention of her name.

But I don't feel either of those feelings right now.

Perhaps this freeing North Carolina mountain air has seeped into me, or maybe it's because I'm finally single, or that I'm happier than I've been in years, or a combination of the three, but I feel excited, anxious, as giddy as one could be.

Uncle Joey pipes in. "Let's show 'em a good time, huh? Did I hear something about a special? Ya got something in mind?"

Friday, August 27

"I got the bathrooms," Uncle Joey says. "You sweep and mop the floors. Let's get this place looking extra spiffy for this evening."

Though I haven't spelled it out for him, Uncle Joey knows, by my anxious body language alone, that this evening is important to me.

"I'm on it. And hey, I saw the specials board...thank you."

Before I even walked in this morning, he had written, "Julie's Crew: Buy 1 Get 1" on the *Specials* chalkboard above the taps. Last night we had talked about doing buy one, get one half off, but he's obviously feeling extra generous.

"Thank you, Emmy. This is our place. If tonight is important to you, it's important to me."

I smile at the mention of "our place." I sweep the floors, mop them with extra care, and scrub the countertops before heading back to the camper to refresh my makeup and clothing. I want to feel good tonight.

I decide I need Louie.

"Hi, Emmy!" Lou answers. "I only got a minute. I'm taking a group of talkative thirteen-year-old girls out on the water in ten."

"Sounds…fun. Listen, really quick, Mabel is coming to the brewery tonight."

"Mabel Pickett? What the hell is she doing in Asheville?"

"A bachelorette party. Mabel's friends are friends with Millie and Jane, so they're all coming here tonight. To the brewery."

"What? I haven't even been to Uncle Joey's brewery. This is nuts! You lesbians all know each other."

She's not entirely wrong.

"Well," she says. "Are you excited? It's been a year at least, right? And you're finally single."

"Fourteen months since I've seen her." Again, I hear how ridiculous the exact number of months sounds coming out of my mouth.

"Oy vey," Louie mumbles. "Is she dating that Naomi girl still?"

"I don't think so. Apparently, she's been seeing a girl named Karen from her law school. I don't think it's serious, though."

"Wow. She must have a thing for lawyers and classmates."

"That's not helping, Lou."

"Well, Karen sounds like a real nerd and not as cool as you. Be yourself. And all that other cheesy advice you already know."

"I'm really excited to see her. That sounds weird, huh?" I don't pause long enough for a response. "I don't even know what I'm expecting of the evening. It's not like we'll magically reconnect and decide to carry on some long-distance love while living nearly four hours from each other."

"Well, she knows she's going to be seeing you, right?"

"Yes," I confirm. "Tobin told me that she told Mabel and Mabel seemed, in Tobin's words, 'cautiously thrilled.' Whatever that means."

"Hmm." Lou ponders the situation a moment before responding. "Well, listen, just be. Just enjoy the evening, whatever comes of it. She might have a girlfriend, she might not. She might be interested in men again. Who knows? I haven't spoken to her in a while. She may have just gotten out of a long relationship and is in no position to pursue any long-lost emotion. So don't put pressure on the situation. No expectations at all, all right?"

"All right," I agree. "No expectations."

"You two had something special. I remember that, so I know this...if you are excited to see her, then regardless of who or what or where she is in her life right now, she is excited to see you too. I'm sure of that."

"You're the best. Thanks, Louie."

"I gotta run now. I love you!" she shouts. I hear her scuffling around behind the phone. "No expectations, ya hear? Call me first thing tomorrow. I'll need all the details!"

She hangs up the phone before I have a chance to say goodbye.

* * *

Millie and Jane are already two beers deep by the time Julie and her posse arrive. Balloons are grouped in gold, confetti, and blush-pink pods around the bar. A banner that reads "SIP, SIP, HOORAY!" hangs above the chalkboard special. I'm bursting with excitement.

Julie walks in first. I only know it's her because she's wearing a sash that reads "Last Hoorah!" and an over-the-top flower crown. She's been drinking. A lot. She screams, "Let's party!" with her hands up as she storms in. I'm looking right past her though, hoping Mabel walks in.

One, two, three, four people enter before Mabel.

Thank God. She's here.

As she walks in, her eyes grab mine. She was looking for me. She knows I was looking for her too, I can tell by the familiar crooked smile that curls up toward her left eye. I instantly walk from around the bar, her energy pulling me forward.

"Hi." I smile, awkwardly stopping just inches from her.

"Hi." She smiles back before wrapping both her arms around my neck as if she couldn't resist for a single moment longer. I want to tell her "I miss you" but release a heavy sigh instead before reaching my arms around her in reciprocation.

And all goes still.

I breathe her in.

And out.

And in once more, before I come to my senses and step away.

"I, uh, I want you to try this pumpkin beer." I could have asked how she has been, or how school is going, but my nerves are fogging my already iffy conversational skills. "I made it special for Louie's wedding."

"Really?" She smiles. "Well, let's do it."

Uncle Joey and I pour pumpkin beers for the girls, and we toast to Julie.

Tobin reaches over the bar and gives me a squeeze. We've been speaking weekly since our sleepover where we discovered we were nothing more than friends. She sends photos of every single new beer she tries along with an in-depth flavor profile analysis and a zero-to-ten ranking system.

"I saw that hug with Mabel," she whispers into my ear.

My eyes widen. "Oh, stop it."

She giggles and sits back with a wink. "This is an eight point seven by the way. Could use a bit more cinnamon in my opinion, but it feels just like a brisk walk down the aisle in autumn. The bride will love it!"

Uncle Joey and I both laugh at her witty remark, before he responds, "That's a B plus, right? We'll take it!"

I see Karen. It must be her because she places her hand on Mabel's knee, and as she does so, Mabel looks up at me. I quickly turn away, but not before Karen hops up to introduce herself.

"I'm Karen."

I wonder if Mabel mentioned me to Karen before coming in tonight. I'm not sure how that conversation would go.

Hey, Karen, two years ago I met a girl from West Virginia. We had a summer fling and well, I just wanted to let you know that we haven't spoken in over a year, but she's going to be the bartender at the brewery tonight in western North Carolina. Small world, eh?

Sounds especially strange working out the conversation in my head. Plus, if Tobin's explanation of their not-so-serious relationship is accurate, then there wouldn't be a point to mention me anyway.

"Hey, Karen." I wipe my hands dry with a loose towel and reach out to shake hers. "I'm Emma."

"This place is awesome," she says with a thin-lipped smile.

I find myself dissecting her. Her dark curly hair is pulled up into a loose bun atop her head. She wears a gold hoop ring in her nose that makes her look edgy. Her jawline, sharp, like her pointed nose. And her golden round eyes are framed with lengthy eyelashes. She's probably smart like Mabel. Much smarter than me.

"You guys are in law school together, right?" I point at Mabel.

Karen looks a little confused. "You two know each other?"

Well, that answers my question of whether Mabel had mentioned me.

Mabel nods, brushing off Karen's comment and directing her curiosity on me. "Tobin told you?" she inquires.

I fling my head back toward Mabel, trying to repress thoughts of that December night in DC when it was my hand on her leg, her hand around my waist. "Yeah, when Tobin was here a couple months back, she filled me in on things."

Tobin chimes in, "I did!" I see Karen's eyes divert to another conversation taking place within the party. She obviously is no longer interested in how, or if, Mabel and I know each other. Mabel, however, hasn't budged from her inquiring gaze. She's likely wondering just how much Tobin had shared with me about her.

"Ah, yes." She grins, finally blinking. "Tobin did mention that she had run into you."

I nod and put on a forced smile to ensure we don't appear awkward.

"Em!" Millie shouts from the other end of the bar, saving me from myself. "Refills!" I hustle over to fulfill needy orders.

The hours pass quickly. When James, another bartender, shows up around eight, I call it a night and join the crew on the other side of the bar. Beer after beer we get rowdier and, without a doubt, more annoying.

Uncle Joey kicks us all out right at ten. "Go on out back, ladies. Time for James and me to clean up."

We head out toward the camper. I light up a bonfire and all the tiki torches, flick on the multicolored string lights that line the camper, and pop open the reserve brewery cooler of stale beers for all to enjoy.

Mabel waves me over and I'm tipsy enough to not only sit beside her, but to move my chair closer to hers.

"This is kinda like Cool Night." Mabel chuckles. Her beer is wrapped tightly in her two hands, her eyes glued to the fire. One by one the embers dance off the logs, only to be gulped up into the ink-black sky. Our first kiss was on Cool Night. I wonder if she is replaying it like I am. Like I have too many times since our summer together.

"Are you changing the world yet, Mabel?"

"Trying."

"You changed my world," I slur without a second thought.

She whips her finger to her mouth. "Hush." She giggles.

Millie has grabbed the plastic fold-up table from the side of the trailer and there's an intense game of beer pong grasping everyone's unruly attention. No one is even noticing Mabel and me.

I grab her finger from her lips and hold it in my hand. "Come visit. Without these people." I went into the night committing to being free and fearless and there's no turning back now.

She ignores my bold request, pulls her finger away, and begins to fill me in on her family before diving into her coming-out story. "I should have done it sooner," she admits. "I should have done it over our summer together." She turns her head from the blazing fire to face me, her freckles radiant against the fire's light. "I remembered you saying at the beach that one evening…ya know, when we were in Chincoteague?" I nod for her to continue. "That I just needed to give them a chance. You were right. They were great. Really great." She turns back toward the fire. "I just wonder if maybe things would have been different with us if I would have come out sooner. Not been so scared of what other people think, ya know?"

I don't reply, but I wonder also.

"Anyhow, I can't believe you just packed up and moved down here," she says, pausing to take another sip of her beer. "You sleepin' in that thing?" she asks, pointing to the trailer.

"Yeah, I love it. It's awesome. Wanna see?"

The two of us hop up. I tell the group I'm showing Mabel the camper, but no one seems to care, not even Karen.

We step inside and Mabel is almost immediately drawn to the picture beside the pull-out bed. The picture she painted for me two summers ago.

"You kept it?" Her cheeks flush with astonishment and maybe a bit of flattery.

"I like it." I shrug.

She spins around the room, taking note of every little detail. She lifts a wooden spoon with a fish carved into the handle, then she brushes her fingers along the titles of seven books stacked on the same shelf as the plates.

"What happened to you and Kate?" She swirls around to make eye contact. "Not together, right?" Maybe Tobin had already filled her in or maybe it's just super obvious from my flirting tonight.

"No. We uh…we were just in different places. You know how it goes."

"Yep," she agrees. "I do know how it goes. Are you seeing anyone?" she inquires as she steps within a breath of me.

I shake my head.

She takes a deep inhale and a deeper exhale. "I want to tell you that I miss you," she says. "I know that's weird, but I've got just enough liquid courage right now to tell you. I miss you."

She reaches her arms around my waist and up my back, gripping the backs of my shoulders firmly with her hands. I wrap my arms around her neck and let her nuzzle her chin between my collar and jaw. Fire rushes up my spine and thighs and every finger and toe.

In this moment, we are summer. Here and gone all at once.

She steps away. I want to pull her back in, but I resist the urge, knowing she isn't mine to pull back in.

"Have you been lighting the candles?" She points to the familiar candlesticks perched in the windowsill. I put two candles in there the day I moved in and haven't touched or lit them since.

"Not once." I shake my head.

"Well, let's light them. Come on." She waves, urging me to move quickly. "I know it's long after sunset, but does God really care?" I chuckle and light each candle.

"And the prayer?" she questions, though it sounds more like a demand.

I rush through the blessing before she promptly follows with, "My least favorite thing about this week was this awful Legal Methods paper I had to write. A real pain in my ass. My absolute favorite part of the week is right now, seeing you, Em." She grabs my hand. "I know I've had a few drinks, but I mean it." She drops my hand and trades her soft confession in for a peppy dose of reality. "And there is no time for you to share because if we're in here a moment longer, they'll all be out there talking shit about how we've disappeared on them."

"Come on, now." She grips my hand once more, tightly, and holds on all the way to the front door, dropping it the moment it opens.

Saturday, August 28

I turn over my phone to see a text from Mabel.

Louie is going to LOVE the pumpkin beer! You are something special, Emma June. I rushed us through last night, but I'm interested in knowing what your favorite and least favorite part of the week was?

I let my heart race for a moment wondering if I should tell her the truth: that seeing her was not just my favorite part of the week, but my favorite part of the whole summer. I remind myself of Karen and decide it's best to leave any daring conversations to Mabel, given that she's the one in a relationship, or whatever she's in.

I respond.

Your approval on the pumpkin beer is my favorite thing! Can't think of a single bad thing. If there was something, I've forgotten.

Mabel sends a smiley face.

I put on a pair of hiking boots, hop in my car and drive about thirty-five miles east to Old Fort, North Carolina. Millie and Jane told me about the Catawba Falls Trail a few weeks back. "Technically," they said, "much of the trail is privately owned and being used to cultivate hydroelectric power, but go early, no one's out looking for ya."

It's early. And it appears the entire trail may or may not be privately owned, but I'm already here and I need sweat and big trees and a task to accomplish. I make my way through a poorly kept but fairly easy mile-and-a-half trek through mossy stones, an old foot bridge with missing planks, and a tree with the letter M carved into it, which I find just absolutely annoying, until I come upon the falls.

A hundred-foot-high waterfall. Water rushing gracefully from rock to rock to the large crystal pool in front of me.

The morning humidity is heavy on my skin. I slip off my shoes and dangle my knees over a ledge, letting the brisk water cool me from my toes up. The quiet takes me back to a time when Mabel and I sat, leg to leg, upon a similar rock, our feet dangling into a similar pool of water.

I recall Mabel putting her hand on my thigh. I feel her right now and my body prickles up as it did way back then.

She knew I wanted her, so she slid her hand up a bit more until it was under my shorts. I recall her glancing around eagerly before urging my body flat against the rock. She swiftly ran her hand up higher, brushing her soft fingertips around my underwear before lifting the lining up and sliding her way inside.

"AHHHHH!" I scream, forcing the dripping desire from my thoughts and body.

What the fuck.

Journal: Saturday, August 28, 2010

I want to show her the sunflower field down off East Street,
the one by the railroad tracks.
She'd love it there.
I want her skin with the morning.
I want coffee
on the covered back porch cuddled under a knit blanket as the snow
falls.
I want the take-off-all-her-clothes date before work.
I want her
to be the one that walks through the door at the end of each day.

SEPTEMBER

Sunday, September 19

"Come and snuggle with us!" Louie insists, patting the empty bed space between her and Max.

The wedding ended at eleven p.m. and a handful of us hopped into a chauffeured black Escalade back to Max and Louie's house to continue the party. Sometime around three a.m. I fell asleep on a blow-up air mattress in their living room. Sometime around three thirty the air mattress deflated.

I feel old this morning.

It's eight a.m. Louie and I are both sporting smudged mascara and loose, hair-sprayed bobby pins. I crawl between them, postponing my long drive back to Asheville.

"Best wedding ever, guys," I say earnestly. "Really amazing."

"Best beer ever," Max declares, still clearly on a high from the magical evening. "And the bottles! Just really awesome, Em. Thank you so much."

"You're welcome," I say, genuinely pleased with their response to the gift.

"You need to move on back here and start up that brewery," Max says.

"Pleeease!" Louie begs, squeezing me close to her.

"I'm serious," Max says. "Everyone was raving about the beer. You got a real talent."

"Well, thank you. It's in the talks. I need some more time under Uncle Joey before I'd feel comfortable taking the big leap."

Louie switches the topic, wanting to cover all the good gossip before I depart. "Was it weird seeing Kate?"

"No," I say genuinely, thinking back to last night. "It really wasn't."

Kate and I had only spoken a handful of times all summer. I texted her in late June when I read a *New York Times* op-ed about New York pushing to legalize same-sex marriage by the close of 2011. I texted her once more in August, just before her soccer season started, to wish her good luck. Other than that, we were too busy moving on to bother one another.

"She gave me a big hug when I saw her," I share. "We even had a drink together. Seems like she's doing well. She said she has a ton of coaching opportunities for next year."

"Good," Louie says. "I was hoping it wouldn't be weird."

"It wasn't at all." I yawn, rubbing the hangover from my eyes. "I did forget how hot she was. Damn."

Max high-fives me. "Still can't believe you got her."

All three of us chuckle.

"She's seeing Chelsea, isn't she?" I ask.

"They must be," Lou says. "Though neither of them has confirmed."

"They seem like they would go well together," I say.

Chelsea is the assistant volleyball coach. She started coaching the year after I graduated so I never knew her well, but Louie met her through Kate and has gotten to know her over the last couple of months.

"How about you?" Lou asks. "Any more news from Mabel?"

"Nooooo." I sigh dramatically, lifting myself from the bed. "We haven't spoken since the bachelorette party."

"Hmm," Louie grumbles. "Well, I'm sure you'll find your way back to each other again soon enough. You always do."

"Oh, stop it." I smile, hoping with every single bit of my being that Louie is right.

"Have you considered reaching out?" she asks.

"I have, of course, but I feel like she should, right?"

"No!" Max interjects. "Where's the fearless Emma that got Kate back in the day. Pull that version out!"

I chuckle. "I've thought about it. Trust me. I just don't know if she's seeing that Karen girl. I mean, I wasn't exactly being nonchalant about my feelings toward her when we last saw each other."

"I dunno," Lou says. "You did say you two were drinking quite a bit at the bachelorette party, maybe her memory of your interaction is vague."

Max interjects. "You need to reach out. If you have questions, ask her the questions. You have nothing to lose."

Lou nods in agreement with her husband. "He kinda has a point. You don't really have anything to lose at this point."

"Yeah, I guess you're right. I'll give it a little more time. It's only been a few weeks since I saw her. I mean what's another couple, right?"

"Lost time, mate!" Max shouts.

Lou agrees with a head nod. "Lost time."

2011

FEBRUARY

Sunday, February 13

I look over at the girl that has just sat down at the barstool next to me. She's wearing a black blazer, black skinny jeans fitted perfectly to her ankle, pointy-toed heels, and round-framed glasses. Glamorous. A stark contrast to my style, though I, too, am wearing nicely fitted skinny jeans. I've just chosen to pair them with an oversized gray Champion sweatshirt and high-top Chuck Taylors. I take a big gulp of my bourbon and ask her out of boredom, "So what brought you out tonight?"

"I was kidnapped and dragged here," she says, making eye contact with me. "How about you?"

"I'm not really sure." I take another swig.

Two hours ago, I was counting the tiny little string light bulbs that are wrapped around the inside of my tiny little trailer and when I reached light bulb eighty-nine, I began contemplating if I should fall asleep (it was 7:04 p.m.) or go grab a solo drink. Both sounded very depressing for a Sunday evening, but I've been feeling a bit depressing, so I chose the latter in hopes that I may stumble across a conversation.

"I'm Emma," I say, holding out my third whiskey for a *cheers*. She lifts her nearly empty wineglass. "I'm Annie." We clink our drinks together and she swigs back the remaining gulp.

"Excuse me." Annie waves over the older woman working the bar. The bartender shifts her head around and Annie motions for "two" with her fingers. A moment later the bartender places two shot glasses of what I believe to be tequila in front of Annie. Annie drinks both, back to back, turns her body toward mine, and asks, "Want to get out of here?"

"Uh." I can't imagine my face is flattering. My lips open slightly. My eyes wide. "Aren't your kidnappers gonna wonder where you are?"

"They'll be fine without me," she says while packing her phone and credit card back into her olive-green leather clutch. She glances up, knowing I'm going to say yes.

"All right then," I say, grabbing my jacket. "Let's go." I cannot believe myself.

We step outside into the frigid cold. "I parked over here." I motion.

"Leave it," she says without looking back at me. "I'm just a few blocks this way." She pulls out a cigarette. "I smoke when I drink," she says. "It's not my most flattering trait, I know."

We're pacing quite fast, but I take a deep gulp of fresh, icy air and reply, "A healthy mix for a good time."

She laughs.

Within minutes we're in front of a swirling glass door. "Home sweet home," she drones while tossing her cigarette to the sidewalk and crunching it beneath her heel.

She greets what I think is the security guard with a friendly nod and a "Hi, Mike," as she walks past him. I wasn't aware of a single building in Asheville that had a doorman. Who is this chick?

I follow her past the elevator, and we sprint up five flights of stairs to door 503. I guess the cigarettes aren't affecting her stamina. Her perfectly toned legs bounced up each step, and I'm on the verge of hyperventilating as we walk inside. She doesn't seem to notice my lack of stamina, or at least she's pretending not to notice. She grabs my hand and drags me to her bedroom. I hardly catch my breath before she starts taking off her shirt.

I follow her lead.

She slips off her shoes and kicks them aside. I do the same. She unbuttons, then I unbutton, until we're both standing naked, staring at one another. My heart is hammering through my chest. Not with nerves, but excitement. It's been over a year since I slept with Kate, and I'm embarrassingly desperate for intimacy.

I move toward her, but she pushes back, guiding me to her bed, clearly needing to take the lead. "I want to do you first," she says.

I let her.

Monday, February 14

The sun stretches in through Annie's frosted floor-to-ceiling windows, prying open my tired eyes.

It takes me a moment to gather my surroundings. Though I don't consider one-night stands a responsible decision, it was probably best that I didn't drive home. I can still feel the knocking of whiskey against my temples. I take a look around Annie's large bedroom. There's a pile of clothes on the floor, another pile draped over the emerald-green velvet chair in the corner, a dozen different wide-brimmed hats scattered over the lampshades and the top of her dresser. She's messy, like Kate messy.

"Tea?" Annie asks. She would be a tea drinker. She's already showered and dressed in high-waisted tweed dress pants, a black turtleneck, and closed-toe pointy heels. The same heels from last night, I think. She's stylish and *Vogue* pretty. Her dark brown hair is pulled into a tight bun accentuating her rosy high cheekbones and though she's only five foot two, five-three at the most, she has a powerful presence.

I reach out for the steaming mug and take it gratefully.

"Happy Valentine's Day," she says without a dash of sincerity.

"Same," I say as I diligently rub my forehead, hoping to relieve the throbbing. "What time is it?"

"Eight thirty."

"Shit." I take a small sip of the piping hot black tea before reaching for my clothes. "I have to go."

"Work?" she asks.

"Yes," I reply while sliding back on my jeans and oversized sweatshirt.

"Where?"

"Holy Local Brewery. Out in Bent Creek." I stand, admiring how impeccably intact she looks before examining my own outfit. I try to shimmy out the wrinkles from my attire that sat in a pile on the floor all night, but there isn't much I can do to up my appearance.

"I know it, yes. I've been there before," she states. "It's been a while, though. I don't leave downtown often."

I don't recall ever seeing her there, but I'm not certain I would have taken the time to notice her. She's far too sophisticated for me, and I'm finding it hard to believe I'm even in the same space as her this morning.

"Are you the brewer or something?" she asks. "Why do you have to be there so early?"

"I brew, I serve, I clean. My uncle owns it. The two of us run it."

Her eyes perk up. I think she's happy to hear that she didn't just sleep with a jobless drunk. She may even be slightly impressed that I'm in close ties with the owner, though she doesn't seem like much of a beer drinker. Just a hunch from the wine last night and the tea this a.m.

"Where do you work?" I ask, curious to know more about this alluring stranger.

"At the Biltmore. I'm the head event planner."

The Biltmore is the single most famous tourist destination in Asheville. The 250-room French Renaissance Château is a marvel through and through, and Annie looks exactly like the type of ritzy persona that would provide the astounding event planning services that one would expect when hosting at the estate.

"Wow. That's a beautiful place to work."

"It is. It's gorgeous," she says. "Have you been?"

"I haven't." I pick up my keys and we both head toward her oversized front door. She opens it for me and locks it behind us.

"I'll take you sometime," she says.

Again, she bypasses the elevator and the two of us hurry down the five flights of stairs to the front door. I'm too focused on trying to keep up to respond to her offer, though I guess this means she's interested in hanging out again. When we finally reach the bottom, she says, "It's a bit formal, but given our tardiness to work, here's my business card."

I look down at the small official greeting, her name stamped in black ink: Annie Bloom. I look up from the card. She's staring at me. "You know," she says. "I've never done that before."

My eyes widen in shock. "You've never slept with a woman!" I say entirely too loud. "You seemed so…well practiced."

"No!" She looks at me like I'm an idiot. "Of course I've slept with women. You're just the first one that's literally a stranger."

My eyebrows perk up, and I must look as dumb as I feel. I'm not sure why, but I think Annie finds my disarray amusing. She leans in and kisses my cheek. Gently, as if she hopes to do it again. "I had fun last night," she says before strutting off in her black wool peacoat.

She's a whole block away before I gather my senses. "I'll call you!" I shout.

Wednesday, February 16

"She's not my type, but I'm lonely, Lou!"

"She was good in bed, wasn't she?" Lou already knows the answer.

"Amazing."

"Well, then call her. You went home with her after a single sentence. I can guarantee she's not looking for anything serious. And if you're not either, then go for it."

"I'm going to call her. I'm calling now. Goodbye."

I take a deep breath and dial the number on the business card that Annie Bloom gave me on Valentine's Day.

"This is Annie," she answers.

"Annie, hi, this is Emma…from the other night."

"Yes, Emma. I remember."

Well, this is a good start. "Do you want to hang out tonight?"

"Yes, any interest in coming to my place?" Annie's voice is soft, sweeter than I can recall from our first encounter. "I can be home by six?"

"Yes! Yeah, that sounds nice. I'll be there."

* * *

Shortly after six, Annie opens the door. It appears she's just thrown her hair into a relaxed high bun but hasn't gotten around to changing out of her tailored dress pants and jacket. In the sober light, I can see that she's older than me. I'd guess midthirties, but it's not her skin that gives her age away. There's an elegance about her. A maturity that takes real life to grow into.

"Your place is nice," I tell her as I throw my jacket atop a dozen others that hang stuffy on the coat rack.

"Thank you."

She's straightened up for our evening. The piles of things that I noticed the other morning are now organized piles of things. Heaps of books on the glass coffee table. Keys, breakfast bars, and stacks of mail lay on the entryway console, and the sink is full of a week's worth of wineglasses. It's a bit too cluttered for my taste, but I imagine this version of organization is what she considers clean.

She flicks on her gas fireplace and picks up a remote that commands the blinds to close halfway down her floor-to-ceiling windows.

"Red or white?" she asks, replacing the remote in her hand with a bottle of each.

"Red."

"So, do you always go solo to the bar?"

My initial instinct is to reply honestly. Yes, I should say. When I'm bored. Lonely. Sexually deprived. Missing home. Yes. I go to the bar alone. But I decide to leave out the theater and answer simply, "Sometimes."

She hands me my glass. "Well, I'm glad you did." Her mildly standoffish parade from Sunday evening has dissipated and replaced itself with a genuine Southern charm. She's thankful for my company if nothing more.

We clink our glasses together. A single sip and I feel myself relax into the moment. "Were your kidnappers mad you left without telling them?"

"No." She smiles. "My friends were thrilled."

"Thrilled? Did they know you took a stranger home?"

"Well, that's kind of what they were hoping for."

"Oh." I raise my eyebrows. "What was the occasion?"

"Well, this is somewhat strange to share right now, but since we've already slept together, it's probably appropriate."

I nod my head, anxious for her to get to the point.

"I officially have an ex-wife as of last Friday."

"Oh. Wow." I take an exceptionally large gulp of wine.

She does the same before carrying on. "We've been separated for a while. She moved back to Charleston, where we're both from, about six months ago and the divorce process was just drawn out due to the distance."

"How are you holding up?" I ask earnestly.

"I'm honestly relieved it's over. I was just…I guess processing it all a bit irresponsibly this weekend."

I clench my jaw and squeeze my eyes at the realization that I was her rebound. I'm not upset, I'm just digesting her comments visually.

"You're upset with me?" She nods as if she expected this type of reaction. "I completely understand if you want to leave. I'm in no place at all to be giving any of myself to someone else right now. I just…I really enjoyed your company. It's frankly been a while since I've hung out with an attractive woman and… and well, if you want to stay, I'd like that."

"I'm not mad and I don't want to leave," I tell her. A smile unravels over my face as I play out how I got to this peculiar moment. Eight months ago, I broke up with my perfectly suitable, beautiful girlfriend. Shoved my college degree under the bed, moved to Asheville to brew beer. I have ridiculous fantasies about a life with Mabel, who, frankly, is as much of a stranger as Annie, and I've just confirmed that I was invited over to this divorced woman's fancy condo to sleep with her. To top it off, I want just as badly to sleep with her, and I'm wondering if this means that I've lost all value and respect for myself.

"What's funny?" She interrupts my thoughts.

"Nothing. Nothing." I pull myself together with another sip of wine. "Honestly, I'm in no place to invest myself either. It's just nice to be here. To be with someone. To be with you."

A soft sigh of relief leaves her red lipstick lips. "Are you hungry?"

She heads to the fridge, but before she opens the door, I chime in. "Do you wanna hook up?"

She spins back around, a playful hunger on her face. "I thought you'd never ask."

MAY

Saturday, May 28

"I've been living here for two years now, and I didn't know the Asheville Tourists existed." Annie brushes a bit of dirt off her windbreaker. Even in sporty gear, she looks proper as could be, her hair in perfect swirls under her blush Nike hat.

"Looks like I finally get to introduce you to something new," I say, pleased with myself, but mostly just thankful we weren't sitting at some parlor sipping Cabernet.

Annie's been dragging me all over town. A wine bar one evening and a facial on another. Barre classes and a musical. Grilled octopus and divine filets. I told Louie I'm finally tapping into the finer things in life and her only question was if I'm still exclusively wearing V-neck T-shirts. Yes is the answer, and much like Lou, Annie makes sure to comment on every single thing I wear in a desperate attempt to broaden my attire. It isn't going great for her.

I have yet to bring her around Millie and Jane. Not for any specific reason, we just haven't lined up a time or reason that feels appropriate, but I've met two of Annie's friends. I find them both, like I find Annie, to be utterly misplaced in this mountain town. Like heels on a hike. There's Courtney, who owns a five-star tapas restaurant in town. And then there's Grace, who manages a high-end boutique retail shop, also in town. Grace seems a bit snobby, but Annie insists it's just her shy nature. Both Courtney and Grace prefer tea over coffee like Annie does. They all get biweekly pedicures and lash extensions. They couldn't care less about the latest crafty beer I brew, and they certainly do not care for any type of sporting event. So, it's no surprise that Annie hasn't been to a Tourists single-A baseball game because Annie doesn't like baseball.

We grab our drafts and take our seats. "So where does your love of baseball derive from?" she asks, already attempting to distract herself from her boredom.

"My dad and mom," I say.

I think of my earliest baseball memories. I was six when I went to my first Major League game. My dad and mom took me to see the Orioles. It was April and it was sunny, and I remember the grass being so green and perfectly trimmed in diagonal rows of dark, then light, then dark again. Black and orange baseball caps and buttoned-up jerseys, drinks spilling, the cheering, the smell of hotdogs and pretzels. I fell in love instantly.

The memories spark a smile. "Look around," I tell her. "What's not to love?"

"I can think of a few things," Annie snarks. "Have you ever dated a woman that actually enjoyed going to these games with you?"

"Is this a date?" There didn't need to be an official announcement to know our two to three hangouts per week classified as dating, though it was a hundred percent clear that this little rendezvous was nothing more than a space saver for the both of us.

"Not a chance," she assures, puckering her lips. "I'm just curious."

I think of Mabel, as I often do when I think of baseball, or wildflowers, or forest-green trucks or summer. "There was a girl once, yes."

Annie rotates her whole body so that she's interrupting my view to the field. "Mmm. Where is this girl? And why do you still love her?"

I shove her playfully back into her seat. "I'm watching the game!"

I can feel her eyes roll as she sips her cider. "Fine. But what is her name?"

"Mabel," I say instantly. It feels good to hear her name on my lips.

"What happened?"

"We just parted ways. It was years ago."

"How long ago?"

"Three summers ago. She wasn't out yet. Bad timing, I guess."

"She's out now?"

"She is out now. Way out. All in the lesbian scene."

Annie laughs. "Everybody has their own timeline. Do you keep in touch at all?"

"No. I actually saw her last August. She was seeing someone, though."

"Oh no, did you make a move and get shot down?"

"No." I let out a giggle, appreciating both her forwardness and her lack of empathy. "No move, but I thought, ya know through our conversations that night, that I made it clear that I was interested. But nothing came of it."

"You never reached out?"

"I was so, so close to calling her a dozen different times after that weekend." I recall scrolling through my contacts to Mabel's name and nearly pressing the call button numerous times. "But I just didn't feel like it was appropriate for me to reach out. I just...I just think I made my intentions clear, and she would have contacted me if she still felt something."

"Clear? How clear? Clear as in telling her verbatim, 'Hey, Mabel, I would like to take you out on a date and then bone you.' That kind of clear?"

I look over at her in annoyance.

"What? If there is one thing I have learned from my divorce, it is to speak. Not in facial expressions that you assume she understands, but in actual, real, clear, assertive sentences."

My eyes widen at her wisdom. "Okay, okay. Perhaps I didn't make myself clear enough. But it's too late now anyhow. It's been a whole year."

"No, you said you saw her in August. So, it's actually only been about nine months. See what I mean about being precise with your words?"

"Okay, Mrs. Therapist," I say without taking my eyes off the field. "How much do I owe you?"

"I'm not your therapist. It would be completely inappropriate for me to be sleeping with my patient." I turn toward her, and she cracks a small smile, which makes us both laugh before she continues in a less serious tone, "What's your hesitation?"

"What's your concern?"

"I'm bored of this game," she whines. "And also I'm interested in you. Come on, tell me. Your therapist is listening."

I chuckle again, turning to face the diamond once more as I contemplate my answer.

"I guess I just worry that I've curated this magical fairy tale of a future together when it probably won't be anything like that, ya know?"

Annie squeezes my hand. "But what if it's exactly like that?"

JUNE

Friday, June 24

Hi Kate! I just saw that New York's Marriage Equality Act was signed into law today! You can officially have your magical, over-the-top wedding at a winery by your parents' house one day. Great news for your home state!

I haven't spoken to Kate since Lou and Max's wedding in September, but in my elated state, it seems appropriate to share in the joy. Less than a minute passes before my phone chimes with her response.

I open her text message to a photo of a princess-cut diamond on a silver band. It's sparkling neatly atop her manicured left hand. *I'm engaged!* she writes. *And I'm already researching top pop cover bands in upstate New York!*

A sharp sting flutters in my heart and then out just as quickly. A dash of jealousy at the unexpected message. She found her person. She has what I want. I let it soak in for a moment before allowing my heart to fill back up with genuine happiness for her. *Congratulations, Kate! That's a beautiful ring. You'll make a beautiful bride.*

Thank you, thank you, she replies.

* * *

"Kate is engaged," Lou says.

It's nine p.m. I'm in bed. "I heard and I'm fine."

"Of course, you are. You're sleeping with Keira Knightley's twin sister, but how in the hell do you know? I know it's not from social media because I send you funny messages weekly and you still haven't responded to a single one."

"I really need to delete social media."

"No," Lou says. "You just need to tune back into your generation, but first tell me how you know?"

"I texted her about New York passing the Marriage Equality Act and she told me. It must have happened this morning?"

"Yeah, it did, and also, congratulations! This is a step in the right direction for our people."

"It is." I chuckle. "And I'm happy for her. It's Chelsea, I assume? The one from your wedding?"

"It is. They're cute, but listen! The real reason I'm calling…I ran into Mabel today."

"Where?" I say, my heartbeat picking up a notch.

"She's home. In Frederick. Max and I had to grab some stuff at Home Depot, and we ran into her there. Her dad apparently had a pretty serious stroke a few months back. Did you know about this?"

"No…I had no idea." I feel sad that I didn't know, but why would I know? "Is he okay?"

"He's fine overall," Lou continues. "Rehabbing and everything, but she's apparently been here all summer and, this is the good part of the story, she is single. And she asked about you."

"That's the good part?" I roll my eyes.

"I feel you rolling your eyes," Lou murmurs. "Yes, Emma. That is the good part. She asked about you! I told her that you and Uncle Joey have been talking about expanding the brewery up this way and that you're crushing it, and that you're excited to start your own thing. I mean, I talked you up. And in case you forgot, you are also single and you still love her!"

I chuckle at her tone—and volume. "I will reach out to her. I appreciate the good vibes. You're a real good pal."

"I am the best pal. You call her, Emma. You call her this time. I'm serious. And you report back. You have one week."

Click.

Saturday, June 25

"Uncle Joey, I was hoping we could talk more about the brewery expansion."

It's been just over a year since I came to Asheville. I miss home. I miss the river, and Louie, and spending Sundays watching baseball with Dad. Plus, I'm good at this whole brewing thing. Uncle Joey has let me in on every trick of the trade, and I feel more ready than ever to venture out on my own.

Uncle Joey doesn't flinch at my request. "You're ready, huh?"

Uncle Joey has known since day one about my dreams to open my own brewery, but after a few months at Holy Local, I pitched the idea of a brewery expansion instead of starting fresh and we've been running with the concept ever since.

I love this brewery. I love the beers. I love working with Uncle Joey. I've been a big part of the distribution growth and I want to be a big part of the future of the company. Plus, it's a bonus that his financial backing will minimize the stress and risk that accompany venturing out.

"I'm ready," I tell him confidently.

"Me too." He grins his electric smile and my insides flutter. "I'm thinking we need to close out these pending distributor deals. That will give you a stronger foothold up north. We can use the rest of the summer to work out the financial needs, and in September we'll lock in a second location."

"You've been thinking a lot about this, huh?" I'm excited he's put real thought into my dreams.

He winks. "I've had some time to mull it over."

"Thank you." I hug him tightly. "I'm gonna crush it up north, and you'll be just as thankful as I am that you're helping me do this," I say with a wink.

He chuckles. "I know you're gonna do great things."

"All right," I tell him. "I gotta go freshen up, I'll be back before noon for my shift."

I strip off my cleaning gear and hop in the shower. The giddiness of my future washes over me. Holy Local Brewing Company North. The thought of running a location solo is equal parts thrilling and daunting, but any hesitations are eased by the comfort of moving back home. I think of my dad, then Louie, which leads me to thoughts of Mabel. I hop out of the shower and text her.

Hi Mabel, Lou told me about your dad. I'm thinking about him. And you. Hope you are well.

Only a moment passes before she responds. I can't open the message quick enough.

Are you home this weekend?

A shiver runs up my spine. I wish I was home. I will be soon.

No, I'm not. I was just talking with Lou on the phone.

My phone starts to ring. It's Mabel. I can't contain the smile that erupts across my face. "Hi."

"I thought I'd just call. It's been a while since I've heard your voice." I can see her half-moon smile on the other end of the phone as I lay down on my bed, towel still wrapped around me.

"It has been a while. How's your dad doing?" I ask.

"He's good, given the circumstance. I dunno how much Lou shared, but his left arm is paralyzed. Permanently, it seems, but he's walking okay. He's got a brace on his leg. Doing rehab every day. His spirits are good."

I feel a stab in my chest as I grapple with the news. "Gosh, how are you doing with everything? I'm sure it's been hard on you and your family."

"It's been okay. My mom is so strong. She hasn't skipped a beat. Picked up all the farm work. Still has the art studio downtown. Still cooks, cleans, and runs the show seamlessly. I've been back in town most of the summer. And my brother's here. He's a trainer over at Rock Fitness now, so he's just down the road from her. She wouldn't ever tell us, but I know she appreciates having the extra hands around to help."

"I'm sure she does. She's lucky to have you two."

"I'm thankful I can be here. It feels good to be home with them. Makes me think about moving back after law school. Ya know this time next year, I'll be done."

"Gosh, time flies, huh? How is school going?" We haven't spoken since last summer yet this conversation feels as natural as a phone call to Lou or my dad.

"It's good overall. I had to take the summer off to help my mom, but I've been working with this non-profit called Love Rules Foundation. I've really enjoyed it. I'm looking forward to getting reengaged when school starts back up. By the way, did you see New York officially legalized gay marriage?"

"I did!"

"It's great, isn't it? All this changing right before our eyes. Maryland is next. The polls say so anyway." I hear a confidence in her voice that wasn't always there.

"I hope so," I tell her.

"Me too."

The line is quiet for a moment. I imagine her radiant eyes peering into the same sky I see from my trailer window, four hundred miles south of her.

"I'm planning on moving back up north soon," I tell her. "Hopefully by the fall or winter at latest."

"You're opening up that brewery finally, aren't ya?"

"I am."

"Lou filled me in a bit. Would love to hear the details. Let me know when you're up this way next time, will ya?"

"I will."

I hear a car door slam and some rustling of plastic bags, groceries, I think. "Hey," she says, sounding distracted. "I gotta run, but it was good hearing your voice, Em."

I chuckle a bit, unconsciously, at how strange it is that I've spent months contemplating whether to text Mabel and when I finally do, she calls. She picks up the phone and calls me and we talk as if it hasn't been eleven months since we last spoke.

"It was good talking to you, Mae. See ya."

JULY

Tuesday, July 12

"You look stunning, Emma."

I'm wearing a black fitted dress. I curled my hair and put a little extra effort into applying my makeup. It's a rare occasion that I look in the mirror and feel so put together, so pretty. Perhaps Annie really is having an impact on me.

"Thank you." I lean in to kiss her cheek before returning the compliment. "So do you."

"So, where are we having this big date?" I ask.

"We're staying here," Annie says.

"Here?" My eyes widen with excitement. "At the Biltmore?"

She reaches for a plastic carryout bag and a bottle of red wine and leads me from her office to a room down the hall.

"You first," she says, waving me through an opened wooden door, which she shuts behind us. We're in a large room with a small wooden table, a single red rose centerpiece, and two brown leather chairs. The fireplace is crackling with fresh pinewood, and there's a Christmas tree decked in red and green and gold bulbs towering over the corner of the room.

"This is one of my favorite rooms." She smiles. "And the only one that gets decorated for Christmas in July."

"It's beautiful," I say, admiring the grand ceiling and architectural details, the garland draped around each window. "How'd you pull this off?"

"I have connections." She winks. "I've always wanted to bring a date here, and well, Emma, you are the one."

"What an honor." I smile genuinely. Our relationship is just as playful and noncommittal as it was on day one. In fact, I'm fairly certain she is seeing someone else due to the overload of text messages she receives from a girl named Eliza, but it doesn't bother me. I appreciate her company, her conversation, her touch. And when I'm not with her, I'm consumed with brewery expansion outlines and thoughts of reconnecting with Mabel when I finally get back up north.

Annie and I spin our forks around our drunken Thai noodles and sip our wine slowly, taking in the unique experience.

"Do you ever see yourself getting married again, Annie?"

"Not a chance."

"You sound so certain."

"I am. My dad is on his fourth wife and my mom has been divorced twice. Marriage just seems so silly. Committing yourself to a single person for all the days of your life…until, of course, you find something better. I've tried it. I failed. It's just not for me."

I think of my parents, how they'd dance together in the kitchen, how my dad would bicker over my mom's grocery list and how my mom would criticize the way my dad folded laundry. I think of how they left each other love notes and how they kissed and how they laughed and how they hugged.

"It must have been hard to go through your divorce," I say, empathizing with her negative view on commitment.

"Eh, I'm over it." She takes another sip of wine. "I'm negative, aren't I?" She smirks and I nod, not agreeing or disagreeing, just letting her know that I appreciate her candor.

"You know," she continues. "There is such a stigma to graduate college, to fall in love, to get married, to buy a house, to have babies. I just kinda...fell into that. What about travel? What about career? What about personal goals? Maybe I'm a little selfish, but I've recommitted myself to my personal needs and freedoms, and I don't really see myself ever wanting to give that up again."

"Well, who is to say you can't do all those things with someone you fall in love with? Maybe the right person will feel just like freedom."

She takes a deep breath, recovering from her passionate rant, and smiles. "Well, maybe you're right. What about you, Emma? What are your thoughts on marriage?"

"I'd like to get married one day."

"What's the appeal?"

"The appeal?" I chuckle. "I mean, it's all very cheesy, but since we're sitting in this romantic little room having a romantic little date, I'll share."

Annie chuckles and crosses her legs to prepare for whatever I am about to share.

"The appeal is having a teammate. For life. Someone that knows the way you like your coffee. Someone that knows your favorite flower and brings them home to you. It's a best friend. Someone to talk to about your dreams and your goals and your ideas and the family you hope to have and when it comes to the real important stuff, you want all the same things. And you bicker, sure, and maybe you're tempted by others, sure, but there isn't a thing in the whole world that could come between the two of you. I want that. That's the appeal."

"Miss Emma! You're so much more romantic than I ever imagined. I'm worried you're wasting your time with me. Have you called Mabel yet?"

"You are not a waste of time, Annie. You've taught me so much about fine dining." I chuckle sarcastically. "And what not to wear."

"Well," Annie says, lifting her wineglass for a toast. "Despite my skepticism of the institution, I think you are going to make a great wife to someone one day."

My insides tingle as they always do when she says something so sweet. It doesn't happen often, so I know she means it.

"Now how about Mabel? Where do you two stand?"

I perk up my eyes, finding it humorous that she's so invested in my status with Mabel.

"Tell me you spoke with her."

"I did. I actually talked to her. Her dad is dealing with some health issues, but I told her when I'm in town next, I will reach out."

"Good." Annie raises her glass and I follow her lead. We toast. "To the good love." She winks. "The kind that knows how you like your coffee."

AUGUST

Tuesday, August 2

My phone beeps and I lift it to see a text message from Mabel.

Did you see this?

I click the attached link and head back to the brewery office to sit down. The link leads to a *New York Times* article about two women, Mary (73) and Sue (74). They've been committed to one another for thirty-one years and they were finally, legally, able to say, "I do."

Mary is quoted, stating, "I get to call her my wife. Wife! It makes me smile just saying it." And another quote farther down the article from Sue reads, "Today is a great day to celebrate love. I've been saying that to Mary for 31 years, but today really is a great day because, today we get to celebrate it with the whole state."

There's a picture of the two of them. Mary's a bit taller, but they're both dressed in white pants and white fitted blazers. Their bobbed hair is gray, but their grins are youthful and stretched ear to ear. Their hands are locked and high up in the air. They're happy.

I put my phone down for a moment and imagine Mary and Sue going home after their courthouse wedding and sitting down in their respective living room chairs and eating strawberry shortcake together or dancing to the FM radio or watching the evening news, all while addressing each other as "wife" enough times to make up for the last three decades.

I text back: *That was really sweet. Thank you for sharing.*

Mabel responds: *How are you? Any plans to come up North?*

I'm good, I text her. *Pretty sure I'll be up at the end of the month. Will you still be around?*

Yes! Would love to see you. I'm planning on heading back to school on September 2.

That would be great. I'll follow up as it nears. Is your dad well? Family good?

All are well. Thank you for asking.

My heart feels light knowing she thought of me this morning as she read the article about two old women in love.

"Emma?" I hear Jane and hurry up from the office to the taproom.

"Hi, guys," I say, running around the bar to give each of them a hug.

Millie holds up a steaming plastic bag and I wave them toward the bar for a seat.

"Yum, thank you for bringing these." I'm nearly drooling as I lift a flakey warm biscuit. "I'm starving," I add. It's nearly eleven a.m.

"Well, we wanted to leave you with a good memory of us." Millie grins. "Here's the jams." She digs through the bag and hands me three small plastic containers. "This one's a blackberry jalapeño, this is a sweet potato, and here's a bourbon maple."

"Spicy it is," I say, digging my knife into the chunky blackberry jalapeño jam. "So you guys leave tomorrow, right?"

Jane took a job in the HR department at Boise State University in Idaho. I'd be depressed over this, but since I'm gearing up to head back north, I'm nothing but elated for their next adventure.

"Yup, first stop on our four-day haul is Kentucky."

"You two will have a blast." I see them smile softly at each other and it makes me think of the article about Mary and Sue. "Mabel sent me this sweet article this morning in the *New York Times*. I'll have to text it over." I hadn't thought twice about using Mabel's name so casually, but their eyes widen at my comment.

"Mabel Pickett? You two talk often?" Millie asks with a curious squint.

They know Mabel and I have a history, one that ended years ago, and our somewhat discreet conversations at the bachelorette party certainly didn't insinuate much, so I'm guessing they probably find it weird that I've just mentioned her name. Especially because they are familiar with Karen.

"No, no, not really, she just texted this morning."

I look up at them and can tell by their strained stares that they are trying really hard to hold in their pestering, but Jane breaks. "I need more."

This makes me giggle before continuing, "She's not with Karen anymore...I mean not that that matters, we're not a thing or anything."

I shrug my shoulders before Millie chimes in, "But you could be!"

I nod my head for the first time in a long time, insinuating that yes, we could be maybe. This makes all three of us chuckle.

"I think I'll see her up north when I go," I say.

"Well," Jane says. "I guess now is a good time to let you know that I saw the hug you two shared at the bachelorette party."

I cover my face with my palm. I didn't think anyone had noticed.

She continues, "I wasn't sure what to think about it at the time, you two seemed a bit...cozy."

She winks, and Millie slaps her leg before interjecting, "You should definitely see her. I don't know her well, obviously, but she seemed really nice and also"—she smirks—"really nice to look at!"

Monday, August 29

"I'm so ready for this move. I'm pumped to get the brewery up and running, and I just feel like I'm missing something down here."

"It's some*one* you're missing." Lou giggles. "And don't worry, you'll see me soon, Emmy."

I chuckle, knowing I walked into that one. "I'm leaving early tomorrow. Like five a.m. I'd leave today, but Annie and I are grabbing a drink at Sol. It's actually the bar we met at back in February."

"Romantic. How are things with you two?"

"We're fine. We have a really great time together, but it's basically over. If it weren't for this move forcing us to part ways, then we'd potentially keep hanging out…I guess…but I'm ninety-nine percent sure she is seeing someone else. We're just friends, really. That occasionally sleep together."

"Well, Emma, that sounds depressing."

Hearing myself say it aloud does, in fact, sound depressing. And also a bit unhealthy, but it doesn't feel depressing. It feels temporary. Kind of like my time in Asheville. "Maybe it is."

"I'm guessing you never called Mabel because I never received my report back."

I don't have time to get into it. "I haven't yet," I lie. "So, are you and Max coming with me to check out the potential new spots?" I ask, impulsively changing subjects. "There's a dozen on the realtor's list. She claims each of them has some real potential. I'm optimistic."

"I am joining, of course, but Max has to work."

I appreciate that she dropped the Mabel topic. I figure if she brings it up in person, we can talk about it more then.

"All right, well, start praying for the perfect building. I would love to lock something in this week so I can get on back home."

"An excellent plan, indeed. See you tomorrow."

* * *

"Now that I actually know you," I tell Annie. "I find it insanely strange that we met in this bar."

Sol Bar is the exact opposite of any place Annie has taken me to over the last six months. Big multicolored bulbs line the drop-down tile ceiling, and a junky jukebox is spinning nineties' pop love songs. I'm drinking whiskey; she's drinking wine out of a plastic-stemmed glass. The lights are low. The bar is quiet.

"I must have been really depressed that weekend, huh?" she says as she peers around the dive bar.

"Thankfully." I wink as we *cheers*.

"Think you'll find the perfect place for your brewery this week?" Annie asks.

"I hope so. It's all Uncle Joey and I have been talking about. We've been working overtime to get things lined up with our distribution and finances. It just feels good to finally take some real steps toward making it a reality."

"Well, I hope you do," Annie says. We sit quiet for a moment, reminiscing on our half-assed relationship over the last six months.

"You know." I look at Annie. "It was an honor to have been your first random bar hookup."

Annie clears her throat. "I'm gonna miss you when you leave this little town."

I can hardly believe it, but I think her eyes are actually glossing over.

"You're crying?"

"Maybe," she whispers before taking a big gulp of her red wine. "My wife cheated on me. That's why we separated."

I place my hand on hers in a gesture of comfort, wondering why she is just now deciding to share this with me.

"Honestly, I wasn't a good wife. Always too busy, too preoccupied to worry about her. Then I met you and you reminded me of how nice it can be to slow down. To just enjoy someone's company." She shrugs her shoulders and smiles softly. "And to have sex again."

I mirror her smile and kiss her cheek.

Annie waves over the bartender. "Two tequilas, please."

This time, instead of taking both shots herself, she slides one over to me, and before we toast, she asks, "Wanna get outta here?"

Wednesday, August 31

"This is it, guys."

I'm sure of it. Dad, Lou, and I have checked out seven other potentials over the last day and a half and I am absolutely certain that this is going to be the second Holy Local Brewery location.

"Frederick, Maryland!" my dad says excitedly, his eyes twinkling like mine.

My mind is racing back to July of 2008. The night on the river with Mabel and Max and Lou, when I dreamt of this moment, this place that I would call my own. Right here in Frederick, Maryland.

"I could build you a bar here," Dad says. "And we could do concrete, like Joey's brewery? Or maybe we do pinewood and line the back wall there with subway tile—maybe black subway tile!"

"And over there you'll keep the kettles." Lou excitedly points. "You could build a big window so we can see the operation through the tasting room."

"We'll have to patch up the brickwork," I say. "And maybe we can add some turquoise and glitter to new concrete floors. What do you think, Dad?"

"A few months and we should have this place up and running, sweetheart."

I do a quick lap around the building and confirm with the realtor that we are a hundred percent in. "This is the spot," I tell her. "This is Holy Local Brewing Company."

The three of us jump into a group hug. "This is the spot, team!" I repeat in utter joy again.

Lou breaks away from the tight grasp. "It's perfect. But now I have to go. Max has instructed that I am to pick up cheeseburgers on my way home. We're so healthy." She winks and scurries off.

I'm more than thankful for Lou's hasty exit. I'm meeting up with Mabel and haven't talked to Lou about it. Not that there is anything to hide, but my own feelings about the meetup are jumbled, so it's best I keep it to myself for now.

Mabel was covering a shift at her mom's art gallery farther up the creek, just a short walk away from the future location of Holy Local. I had shared with her that our last two properties were in Frederick, so she said she'd hang around downtown until I was finished so that we could grab a drink.

"I'm gonna meet with a friend, Dad."

"All right, Em. I can still expect ya home at some point?"

"Yeah, I won't be too late."

I leave my car parked in the future Holy Local lot and follow the walking path along the creek toward Market Street and down East Patrick, where I find Mabel sitting alone at the bar in JoJo's Tavern. She hops up instantly and pulls out the stool beside her.

"Are we doing Bohs?" she asks. "Or are we too old for that class of beer now?"

"I haven't had one since college, but I'm in if you're in."

She orders two and we toast. "To Holy Local Brewery" she says. A quick sip and she begs to be filled in on the property hunt. "Tell me you've found a place here in Frederick?"

I smile widely and spill all about the charming location just down the street from where we are sitting. She's thrilled it's in Frederick and raves about the expanding downtown. We talk about her family and her plans to move home after law school. She asks about Millie and Jane, and I tell her that they've already promised to fly in from Boise to see the brewery when we get the doors open. We even chat about Karen.

"Well, I'm ashamed to admit this…" Mabel's expression is on the verge of laughter. "But we didn't exactly hit it off, mentally. It was more of a…a physical thing that kept me around. I know that's bad." She presses her face into her hands. I laugh at her as I recall my eerily similar relationship with Annie.

Two beers and three hours pass before I peer down at my watch and notice it's nearly nine o'clock.

"You've got to go?" she says, but she knows.

I bite my bottom lip, wanting desperately to say no and stay, but responsibility prevails. "I've got an hour drive back to Alexandria and a long haul back to Bent Creek tomorrow morning."

"It's always too short with you, Emma June," she says as she swigs back the final ounce of her drink.

I smile at her, soaking her in as I did three summers ago at Pickle's Pub. I think of all the evenings I spent wishing for another moment with her. Another moment just like this one.

"When do you head back to school again?" I ask her as I gather my things.

"Friday. Classes start Tuesday."

I nod in response, unsure of how to prolong the conversation but not wanting it to end.

"You think you'll be up and running by November? I'll be home for Thanksgiving."

"Might be cutting it a little close with permits and all, but the challenge is accepted."

She chuckles. "Good. Let me walk you to your car."

We walk side by side up the path toward the empty brewery parking lot where my Jeep awaits me. I feel desire ball up in my stomach and flutter like wild geese through my limbs.

Do we kiss? I want to kiss her.

"This is you," she says as we near the driver-side door.

"You're parked by the gallery, I assume?"

She nods and unexpectedly wraps both of her arms around my waist, letting herself drop into me. Her face is nuzzled in my neck as she's done many times before.

She feels just like home.

"I've been waiting to hug you again for an entire year." Her words are muffled, her breath warm against my skin.

I hold her tight, and we just stand. We just stand under the warm August sky and we hold each other, and I think of how badly I want to hold her just like this tomorrow. And the next day. And every day after. A few deep breaths pass before she gently removes her arms and steps back.

"See ya, Emma June. November, okay?"

I nod in agreement. "November."

NOVEMBER

Friday, November 18

"Emma, honey!" Dad shouts from the open garage doors of the brewery. It's a mild sixty-three-degree day. Not a gust of wind, not a cloud in the sky. I hurry to the taproom from the back office where I've been shuffling through piles of permit paperwork.

"Thanks for stopping by, Dad."

"Of course, sweetie. It looks absolutely amazing in here."

"Couldn't have done it without you."

We both take a moment to scan the open room, admiring the exhausting amount of work we've put in over the last two-plus months. Every single waking hour was spent here. Dad took time off work, Uncle Joey made two separate trips, and we were exceptionally fortunate to find a brilliant contracting crew that worked tirelessly.

Other than the brewery name and the beers on tap, my space is quite different than Uncle Joey's. It's very much my own.

The concrete floors are drizzled with lightning strikes of turquoise and glitter. Dad built a beautiful pine bar that stretches nearly the entire width of the room, and he and a few of his buddies handcrafted eight iron rod taproom tables with concrete tops. Uncle Joey and I didn't pay a penny for them. A gift from Dad. I've decorated each with a tiny glass milk jug and a single yellow sunflower. I thought he'd like that.

We ended up going with a matte black sink and taps. White subway tiles line the back wall, shaping the floor-to-ceiling windows that peer into the brewer's room that houses six new stainless steel kettles and one stunning copper kettle hand-me-down from Dad. Fortunately, the brewing room didn't need any work, so we were able to start preparing beers on day one. It was just the taproom that needed a physical facelift.

We draped café lighting along the ceiling, and my absolute favorite touch is the forest-green draft list that resembles a scoreboard. The top of the board features a replica of the clock that sits above the scoreboard at Camden Yards Stadium. The real clock reads "B-A-L-T-I-M-O-R-E-S-U-N" in place of the standard hour numbers, but ours reads "F-R-E-D-E-R-I-C-K-M-D-!"

"Cannot believe tomorrow is your opening day," Dad says. "You feel ready?"

"I do." I look at him with a fueled grin of confidence. "Hey, there's one last touch. I wanted you to be the first to see."

We head toward the wall just left of the garage doors, and I shove two massive marketing banners aside, revealing block lettering, stamped in black ink on the brick.

Just be happy. Choose happiness.
Above all else. Always.
Drink beer. Not too much.
Watch baseball.
Grow sunflowers.
Be in love. Love rules.
Life is good.
Life is real, real good.
Remember that, will ya?

Dad takes a step back, his brown eyes puffy in awe, in love, as he appears to recall the letter his late wife wrote to their only daughter so, so many years ago.

"This is…this is perfect, Emma. Gosh, this just makes me happy." He pulls me in for a side hug, not able to take his eyes off the words.

I wiggle out of his grip and hustle over to the shelves by the bar. I pull out an XL heather-gray baseball tee with navy sleeves that reads in white print:

Beer.
Baseball.
Sunflowers.
Love.

"I love it!" Dad exclaims. His cheeks are flushed, overwhelmed with pure pride and joy.

I flip the shirt over to showcase the back. Holy Local Brewing Co. is stamped as a last name would be on a jersey and the numbers 00 are large and centered, representing the year 2000, when Uncle Joey first opened the original Holy Local Brewery in Bent Creek.

"I got fifty to start with," I say. "This one's yours." I toss it to him, and he immediately holds it up to his chest for size.

I continue, "And I got these stickers made. Two hundred fifty that say the same thing as the shirts, and another two-fifty that say Holy Local Brewing. We'll sell the shirts for twenty-five dollars, and I want every single visitor that comes through that door tomorrow to get a free sticker."

"It's a brilliant idea," Dad says.

"I can't take all the credit. Uncle Joey had a lot of insight."

"Tomorrow is gonna be great, Emma June. I just know Mom is beaming right now. I'm so proud of you."

"Thanks, Dad. Now come on back here, I want you to meet some of the team."

Saturday, November 19

"What a night, right?" Blake, one of my employees, stretches his hands high over his head to relieve the tension that's built up in his lower back from running around all night.

I can relate. Every bone in my body is basking in exhaustion and joy. Opening day was phenomenal. We had a bigger crowd than I expected for a Saturday soft opening. We didn't do an ounce of advertising and we were only open from noon to five, but somehow a constant flow of friends, family, and strangers kept the front door swinging. We probably could have used another staff member and we had a little hiccup with a broken tap feeding the Potomac Pale Ale, but all was managed as well as could be expected.

"I feel really good about it, Blake. You and the rest of the team were so awesome tonight. Thank you for your hard work."

Blake flips off his Holy Local trucker hat and bows dramatically in appreciation.

"Hey, Emma!" Maria, another employee, yells in from the taproom. "A reporter is here to chat. Want me to let her in?"

I peer down at my watch; 7:43 p.m. The brewery has been closed for nearly three hours. "She's a little late for an unexpected interview," I whisper to Blake. He peeks out of the office and through the brew room windows toward the front door. He shrugs his shoulders. I toss him an envelope of his cash tips. "You're free to go. See ya tomorrow."

I lift my tired legs from my office chair and head out toward the front, hollering back at Maria, "Yeah, Maria, let her in! I'm coming!" As I turn the corner, I see her, more beautiful than ever.

"Hey, stranger." Mabel's eyes sparkling with delight.

"Reporter, huh?"

She lifts her pen and pad, proving her job title before we hesitantly embrace.

"Here, Maria." I hand her an envelope filled with her share of the cash tips. "You did awesome tonight. I'll see you tomorrow."

"Thanks, boss."

I lock the door behind Maria before leading Mabel back toward the bar for a seat.

The only lighting left is the dull café bulbs draped along the ceiling. The music is off. The garage doors are closed. It's quiet. Just the two of us.

"Taps are cleaned for the night, but I have some cans. Do you want one?"

"If you'll have one with me," she says, sliding out a stool. I head behind the bar and open the fridge under the pinewood bar to lift out two Garage Blues.

"It's our winter ale," I tell her. "Planning on putting it on tap in December."

We crack them open and *cheers*.

"I thought you weren't getting back into town until tomorrow?"

The two of us have shared a few dozen text messages over the last few months. An article here, a check-in there. All platonic, but enough to keep me wanting more. So much more.

"I was able to sneak away. Was hoping to get here earlier, actually. Wasn't sure I was going to catch you."

"Well, it's good to see you." I smile. "So, fill me in. What's with the pen and paper?"

She clears her throat. "I'm the reporter, Miss Emma June. I am the one who asks the questions. Now you are still Miss, not Mrs....right?"

"Right." I nod with a slight smile and a roll of my eyes.

"Okay, okay. Now I'm working for *The Femme*. Heard of it?"

I shake my head no.

"It's a weekly magazine. We feature powerful, successful women in and around Frederick and you, Miss Emma June, are my assigned feature this week."

"What an honor." I shrug, sipping my beer.

She smiles and looks at me with her sultry gaze a few moments longer than a friend would. She puts down her pen and loses the forced reporter persona. "This is amazing, Em. Really, really amazing."

"Thank you," I say genuinely. "I'm proud of it."

"You should be. You look great. Happy. I'm proud of you."

I feel myself blush, so I pick up a rag and start to wipe down the already clean countertops in an attempt to distract myself. "So, tell me how you're writing for this magazine in Frederick while going to law school in Durham?"

She chuckles. "It's freelance. I did a few articles for them this past summer while I was around, and I offered to pick this one up since I'm home for Thanksgiving break and I have an insider's connection." She winks.

"Insider's connection, huh?" I repeat with a giddy smile.

"Yes, now will ya come sit over here and chat with me a moment?"

I grab my beer and sit on the other side of the bar in the stool next to her.

We zip through a list of questions that include:

"What drew you to Frederick?"

"What influences your beer offerings?"

"Where did you come up with the name Holy Local?"

And her list goes on until she takes note of the passage printed on the wall to the left of her.

I watch her read it. Her eyes lift, her memory fires up. "I remember these words. Your mom's note?" she asks, wanting confirmation.

I nod, and every freckle on her face curls up with her lips.

"She must be so proud of you."

"I think she is. I hope so, anyway."

Mabel closes her notebook full of chicken scratch and swirls her barstool to face mine. "Can I take a picture of you?"

My eyes widen in question.

"Please don't say no. I need it," she whines. "For the article."

I've never said no to her a single time, and I don't expect to start today.

"How about by the quote on the wall?" she suggests.

"Sure," I tell her. I've got on my Holy Local baseball tee. My hair is pulled into a neat high bun, and since it was opening day, I even did my makeup.

Mabel snaps a few pictures, peers down at her Canon camera, and back up at me. "Beautiful."

My insides shiver.

"Do you wanna go on a date with me?" she asks abruptly.

"Yes, I want to go on a date with you." I have never been more sure of anything.

Mabel shakes her head, thrilled with my response. "Okay, okay, when?"

"We're closed Monday. Does that work for you?"

"Monday it is. Want me to pick you up here?"

"I'm actually renting an apartment right down the street. On East Patrick, above the Co-op Market."

"I'll pick you up there then. Eight a.m.?"

"See ya then."

Monday, November 21

I hop up into Mabel's old pickup truck at eight sharp. "I'm so happy you still have this thing." The door squeaks lovingly as I pull it shut. I sink back into the springy cushion, letting every summer afternoon that we spent cruising around Shepherdstown soak through me.

"Old faithful." Mabel grins as she caresses the steering wheel.

Her hair is braided and hanging loosely over her right shoulder. She's wearing a gray O's cap that I don't recognize, but she feels as familiar as summer.

"That coffee is for you."

I reach down to grab the steaming thermos. "Thank you."

"So, you may have already guessed..." She looks over at me with a curious glare. "We're going for a hike."

"Really? I had no idea." Mabel sent a text last night telling me to bundle up and wear hiking shoes.

"Listen here." She points to the CD slot as if I need to see her press play to hear the music. "Mr. Jones" begins, and we share a quick glance. "It's been in here since our little summer fling." She winks playfully.

"No way!"

"Seriously." Her face straightens up. "I haven't taken it out. I mean I haven't been listening to it on repeat since 2008, but sometimes I do. I like the album. It makes me think of you."

I don't reply. I watch her gentle hands against the steering wheel, the way her eyes blink and refocus under her aviators.

"I missed ya, Em. Really." She glances over to catch my reaction. I smile softly, and she continues, "I'm glad you're here."

We drive forty minutes west to Shepherdstown and park at the C&O Canal Lot, just under the bridge. "For old time's sake," she says, then grins.

We walk side by side along the busy river under canopies of burnt reds and oranges. I fill Mabel in on some of the hikes I took during my time down in Asheville and she talks about a wild sailing experience she had during a thunderstorm on Casco Bay in Maine. She asks what my favorite beer is that I've ever brewed, and I list off four. It's too tough to choose just one. She talks about the Love Rules Foundation she's reconnected with since returning to campus and assures me that Maine, Maryland, and Washington are next on the list to legalize marriage equality. "It'll be on the ballots this time next year," she says. "I know it'll pass."

She's the same, but different. When we first met, there was a tentativeness about her. Perhaps it was that she was unsure about what she wanted to do with her life. Unsure about whether she wanted to date a woman. Unsure of what her family and friends would think. I can't quite pinpoint it, but whatever it was, it's not in her anymore. She's three and a half years older, more educated, more comfortable in her skin.

In this moment, wind striking our reddened cheeks, our feet hustling beneath us, trying to catch up on all this lost time, I find myself in complete disbelief that she is even better now than I remember.

* * *

"Gosh I miss this place." Mabel plops her things down in the window booth of the Sweet Shoppe.

"Me too." I'm elated to sip my old favorite blend and try whatever knickknack they feature in the bakery case. Other than not recognizing any of the employees, the shop looks exactly as I left it. Charming. Poised. Delicious.

We grab two coffees, and a cinnamon roll and blueberry scone to split.

Mabel places down her mug and hurries off to the bathroom. "I'll be right back."

Her phone beeps, lighting up. I don't have to look hard to see it's a message from Naomi. *Are you around?* it reads.

Naomi? The one she dated before Karen?

Mabel's phone beeps again.

I love you.

The text sends a bullet through my chest.

Are they together?

I clutch my hands firmly together in an attempt to stabilize my emotions.

The phone beeps once more.

Call me. Please.

I quickly flip Mabel's phone over before she comes skipping out of the bathroom. I feel disheveled. Pins and needles are pricking down my spine. I don't want Mabel to know that I saw her messages, but I'm struggling to stay composed. I try to breathe deep, but I'm not able to find composure.

I need to leave.

I can't be here in this coffee shop right now. I can't spend another three years imagining a life with her. I feel silly for even spending my day off with her. There is endless work to do at the brewery. I should be there. I own a business. That's my priority. Not this…this stranger.

"How's the coffee?" she asks in her sincere, raspy voice.

"It's great, but I, uh, I actually have to go. You think you can drop me back off at my place? I just remembered I gotta handle something at the brewery."

I think I sound calm, normal, but my thoughts are frenzied, so I'm not certain.

"Of course." She hastily gathers her things, slipping her phone into her pocket without noticing her text messages. "Is there something I can help you with?" she asks as we hop back into her truck. "I'm not doing anything all evening. I'd be happy to help if you need an extra hand."

"No, no, I got it," I tell her. I should just ask her about the messages, but it's none of my business. And I don't want her thinking I was snooping on her phone.

She glances over at me, but I avoid eye contact.

"Is there something wrong?" Confusion cripples her spirit.

"No," I say firmly. "Not at all, I'm just…I'm distracted."

"Okay."

It's a quiet ride back. When we finally pull onto East Patrick Street, she breaks the silence. "I'd really like to see you again, Em."

"Yeah." I nod as she pulls over for me to safely hop out. "Yeah, that'd be nice. I'll call you." I fling my backpack over my shoulder, shut the squeaky truck door behind me, and hurry into my apartment without a look back.

Within twenty minutes, she texts me. My head has been buried in a fuzzy throw pillow since I walked into my apartment. I've been absorbing the fact that I love her. I still love her. I've always loved her, and she is clearly in a relationship with Naomi. Or maybe she's not, but Naomi is in her life. Naomi loves her and Naomi lives in Durham, which is where Mabel will be heading after Thanksgiving ends and I will still be here. Alone.

You saw my text messages? Mabel wrote.

I can't respond. I power off my phone. I toss and turn all night.

Friday, November 25

"Mabel! Hi!" I hear Lou's vigor echo from the bar where she is working, through the brew room, and into the office where I'm sitting. "How are you?" she shouts.

I peak out of the office and catch a glimpse of Lou running from behind the bar to hug Mabel.

Lou is my favorite employee. She works as often as I need her to, as long as it doesn't interfere with her full-time job at the river. The customers are drawn to her magical spark, and she carries herself as if she's invested her life savings into the brewery. I'm fortunate to have such a loyal friend.

I join them in the taproom. Lou looks utterly confused when I calmly approach the two of them. "Hi, Mae."

Lou is in the dark when it comes to Mabel and me, but as she steps aside to examine the dynamic between the two of us, I see her wheels turning. When she can't quite figure out our situation, she shakes her head in confusion and says, "All right, then, I'll give you two a minute."

I offer a fake smile, urging her back behind the bar. She does so without hesitation.

"Can we talk for a moment?" Mabel asks.

It's twelve thirty in the afternoon, we've just opened, and there's only one couple in the corner of the taproom slowly sipping through a pipeline of tasters.

"Sure," I tell her. "Let's step outside."

"Em," Mabel says as we step into the brisk afternoon. "I know why you're upset. You saw the text from Naomi, right?"

"Yeah," I say in an annoyed tone, but I'm not annoyed. Not at all. I was on Monday, sure, but now, seeing her here, I feel silly that I've wasted three whole days ignoring her phone calls and texts. However, I don't let on that my sadness has diffused. "Are you seeing her?" I ask sternly.

"No!" She looks at me and shakes her head in a cluster of distress and frustration. "You could have asked me this the other day instead of giving me the...the silent treatment." She hesitates, her ocean eyes demanding my absolute attention. "Who even cares if I was seeing her? Or if I am seeing her? You and I aren't together, Em! We went on a date. One date! For the first time in three and a half years and I...I guess I thought that we were having a good time. I'm just really not sure why a ridiculous text message that you know nothing about would cause you to end our perfectly good afternoon so abruptly."

I'm drowning in her, consumed with her disappointment but trying desperately to stay committed to my strict composure. "Why did you come here, Mabel?"

"I'm upset! I'm upset that you didn't have the decency to respond to my phone calls or text messages." Her voice is soft, but straining. "I'm upset that you didn't give me the opportunity to explain the situation." She breaks eye contact, defeated. "I am upset that I've spent all these years thinking about you."

My heart hits the soles of my feet, grounding me in this emotional whirlwind.

"I'm sorry," I tell her earnestly. She lifts her eyes to meet mine. "I've thought about you too. Most days...since the moment you drove away from my apartment over three years ago."

"Why were you in such a hurry to walk away from me again, then?"

"Well, it was you that actually drove away from me," I remind her with a smirk.

A smile unravels across her face, alleviating the tension a bit. "You know what I mean," she grumbles.

I step back from her. I need to tell her exactly what I'm feeling. What I've been feeling.

"Listen, this is gonna sound nuts, but I've imagined a whole life with you, Mae. It's crazy. I'm crazy." I can't believe these words are spilling from my lips. "So, when I saw the message from Naomi, it just reminded me that the imaginary relationship with you that I've played out a million too many times, isn't real." I inhale sharply. "I overreacted, I know. I have known since I left your truck. I didn't want to leave you. Not at all. I just…I can't wrap my head around you, around allowing myself to enjoy time with you because…because you're not just another date to me."

She pulls me in and wraps her arms around me tightly. I breathe her in, letting the world silence around us. "I'm not seeing her," Mabel says as she releases me. "We broke up a long time ago. She cheated on me, actually. That's what ended it. Just before school let out this past summer, she asked to hang out again. Karen and I had called, whatever we were doing, quits, so I said sure. Thinking maybe she had just made a mistake and maybe there was still something between us, but nothing came of it. The feelings just weren't there for me any longer. I truly don't know why she texted me. We haven't spoken in months. She claims to have been day-drinking and apologized, but I've asked her not to reach out again."

"I should have let you explain yourself on Monday. I'm sorry."

Her clenched jaw tells me she's still a bit disappointed with me. "I gotta go," she says, shoving her hands in her corduroy jacket pockets. "I won't be back for a while. Probably not until May, after graduation."

"You're leaving for Durham now?" I ask, confused at why she would have to head back to school on a Friday when classes can't possibly start until Monday.

"There's a fundraiser tomorrow for the Love Rules Foundation that I volunteered for months ago."

I nod. "Oh, okay. You're not coming home for Christmas?"

She shakes her head. "I'm going to the Middle East," she says. "Israel, Jordan, and Egypt."

"Oh, wow." That's not what I was expecting to hear. "For school or fun?"

"Work actually. I'm going with a few coworkers through the Love Rules Foundation. They have a sister office in Tel Aviv. While we're over there, we figured we'd check out a couple of the neighboring countries."

"Wow, that's...that's amazing."

"Yeah." She hasn't taken her eyes from mine. "I'm looking forward to it."

We stare silently, six months standing between this moment and the next time we'll see each other.

"Well, I better get back inside," I tell her, wondering if this is how we'll always be. A glimpse, a moment. Entire lives lived in between our defining brief visits.

Mabel leans in and presses her gentle lips against my cheek. "It wasn't just a date for me either." She smiles as she pulls back. My soul warms.

"What's another six months after all this time anyway?" she asks.

Too long, I think, but I save the depressing thought for myself. "See ya, Mae," I say as she spins off down the path toward her car.

* * *

Lou is tapping her fingertips against the quiet bar. Another three customers have made their way to a table, one with a line of tasters, the others with drafts.

"Spill. Now," Lou says sternly as I join her behind the bar.

"All right, all right." I crumble. "I should have told you. We connected back in August."

"When you were in town? When we found this place?" Lou's face is shocked, not in anger but in excitement for whatever I am about to say next. She can't resist a good love story.

"Yeah, briefly. And we hung out again on Monday."

"And…"

I don't feel like reliving the ridiculous text message fiasco, so I don't. "And it was great," I tell Lou. "She's great."

Lou dramatically presses her hands against her heart. "I'm so happy!"

"Oh, stop." I'm blushing. Lou can't get enough.

"So, what's next?" she asks.

"I dunno. She said she's moving back after law school to study for the bar and figure out her next move, so I guess we'll see."

"What?" she says entirely too loudly. "I have to wait a whole half a year for this to play out? Ugh!" She presses her hand against her head as if my love life has just given her a horrid migraine.

"Carry on," she says, waving me back to my office. "I can handle the taproom. Can you please go get the permit done for the live music? I'm getting bored working here."

Sunday, November 27

"Good morning, sunshine!" Lou barges into the taproom carrying this week's edition of *The Femme*. She drops the paper magazine on the bar and hands both my dad and me a piping hot black coffee from Dublin Roasters, the coffee shop just down the street. "Here, drink these," she insists.

We both obey. Sundays are early mornings at Holy Local. My dad comes in to assist with the brewing from seven until opening at noon, and Lou joins us for the first couple of hours to do a deep clean before heading to work at the river.

"I've got us a must-read this morning!" Lou lifts the paper and opens it to page three. Both Dad and I step beside her to admire the full-page photo that Mabel took of me last Sunday evening. On page four there is a smaller picture of the taproom, encompassed by text.

Lou skips to the bottom of the article and reads enthusiastically. "*She's just twenty-four years old, but Emma Sloane carries herself with the steadiness and charm of a seasoned entrepreneur. She sports a simple style, which matches her mild mannerisms, but she has hazel eyes that burn like a bonfire in June.*"

Before continuing, Lou presses her free hand to heart as if she is falling in love with the words.

"When asked what provoked this gigantic undertaking at such a young age, Emma points to the block words, stamped into the taproom wall.

Choose happiness.
Above all else.
Always.

"'It doesn't really seem like that big of thing. I'm happy,' she says as her eyes dance around the room. 'This place makes me happy. Happiness drives me. It moves me. Keeps me going.'

"The words etched on the wall come from a note that Emma's mother wrote to her in the winter of '98, days before she passed away of breast cancer. Emma was just eleven years old.

"'I miss her,' Emma says. 'But I know she's watching over me and my Dad. She's proud, I think, of what we've built here.'

"She is undoubtedly proud. And we here at The Femme *are proud to welcome Emma Sloane as our newest addition to the women business owners of Frederick, Maryland."*

Lou slams the pages closed, and both she and my dad whip their heads around to face me.

"She loves you!" Lou shouts.

"Wait, who is *she*?" My Dad is lost.

I ignore his question and address Lou instead. "Stop it, Lou. She just wrote a nice article."

"Who is she?" Dad asks again, with more angst in his tone.

Lou swings the magazine back open to page three and points at the byline. "Mabel Pickett, Mr. Sloane. Duh!"

I see my dad mentally connecting the dots. "Wait. Mabel? From college, Mabel?"

"Yes, Dad." I nod, simultaneously giving Lou a dirty look.

A slight grinch-like smile draws out across his face. "I liked her."

"So does Emma," Lou says with certainty as she heads nonchalantly back to the utility closet to gather her cleaning supplies.

2012

JANUARY

Monday, January 23

"You can tell me to mind my own business, but are you dating Mabel?"

The brewery is closed on Mondays, but this afternoon, while Dad, Lou, Max, and I were patching up some overdue brick work, a delivery woman with a blossoming bouquet of sunflowers knocked on the door. They were from Mabel, with a note that read: *Happy Birthday, Em!*

"Dad!" I cry. "It's my birthday, do we have to talk about this?"

The four of us decided to stick around the brewery post-brick work, to celebrate my otherwise lame twenty-fifth birthday. Louie called in takeout sushi and we're three beers into our freshest release: Santa's on Vacation. It's a key lime IPA with lactose. A mild hoppy sipper, idyllic for the ruthless post-holiday depression.

Louie waves her pointer finger strictly. "No. No. No! None of that, Emma Sloane. Your dad has asked a valid question, and whether it's your birthday or not, I think we all deserve some answers."

"Oh, please, you two," I whine. "Max, would you like to put in your two cents on this as well?"

"Honestly, I've been wondering since the flower delivery, so yes, I'd also like some clarity."

I give him a dirty look of disappointment for speaking his mind. He finds this humorous.

"I have no time to even think about dating. You guys know that. I practically live here." I throw my hands up, insinuating (with an extra dose of tipsy self-assurance) that this brewery hasn't been running seamlessly without every ounce of my time and effort.

"She's not wrong," Lou says, addressing my dad. "I mean, she even slept in the office that one night, which I still find very strange since she lives a block away."

"It was one time, Lou. Let it go. Also, I live like three blocks."

Dad interrupts our banter. "I'm probably overstepping here, but I liked her. You guys had a thing once, right? Where has she been?"

Lou's eyes erupt with fireworks, gasping for air, shocked that my dad not only brought up the infamous Mabel, but then shared that he *liked* her.

Dad's unwarranted approval of Mabel is enough to move my smile ear to ear. "She's still in school," I tell him. I recall the string of text messages that have been pouring in from Mabel since the day after Thanksgiving. "We're kind of a thing, maybe. It's early. She won't even be home until May, so I'm just trying not to occupy my time with it right now."

Lou coughs up her beer obnoxiously. "Well, you're doing a poor job. You're glued to that phone."

I roll my eyes at her. "I am not."

"You are. You two are obsessed with each other. You always have been."

I press my hand against my face, wishing away the center of attention.

"Well, while we're on the topic of your future love life," Dad says. Wish not granted. "I was just reading today that Governor O'Malley introduced a same-sex marriage bill. Have you guys heard?"

I heard from Mabel, but I display ignorance. I can see that Dad is excited to share this spotlight moment.

He continues, "His administration attempted to propose the bill last year. It failed, obviously, but it sounds like they've clarified some religious protections this time around, and according to what I read, O'Malley is feeling good about it."

Max lifts his pint and demands a toast. "To love for all!" he shouts as we clink our glasses together.

"I hope so," Dad continues. His earnest response reminds me of how fortunate I am to have him. "I was talking to Jim about it today." He looks toward Louie and Max to clarify. "Jim is one of my longtime employees. He and his partner have been together for nine years and they live here in Maryland." Dad leans back, reintroducing me to the conversation. "Anyway, Jim asked for a day off next week to go lobby the delegates, and I'm going to join him."

Lou chimes in. "Can I come too?"

"Yes!" Dad is exhilarated by the opportunity to take real action.

Lou isn't smiling with him, though. She seems confused. "I guess I'm glad that we're moving in the right direction, but is it just me, or is this insane? We are essentially going to beg people in power to vote yes, so that two grown-ass adults that love each other can get legally married?"

Dad looks shocked. "You know, I've never thought about it like that. I've just been thrilled with the progress, but it is pretty nuts that these discussions even have to take place."

"What a birthday discussion, huh?" I say, and the tense chatter dissolves in laughter. "I think it's great what you're doing, Dad." I hold up my pint for another toast. "The gays of Maryland are lucky to have you three advocates."

FEBRUARY

Saturday, February 18

It's nearing midnight. The Edison light hanging from my bedside ceiling is still on, casting shadows along the exposed brick wall in my bedroom. I need to sleep, but like every other night since Thanksgiving, it's too hard to say goodbye to Mabel and face an entire night's rest without her voice beside me.

"I know it's none of my business," Mabel says over the phone. "But we've never talked about it before, and I'm curious to know, are you dating around at all?"

"With all my spare time?" I huff, humored by the idea. "You're the first person I talk to in the morning and the last I talk to before I sleep. No, I'm not dating around. Nor do I have any interest in seeing anyone until I see you."

I hear her sigh in relief.

"I wish I was with you."

I stretch my tired arm across my olive-green duvet and caress the empty space beside me. "I wish you were here too."

"Remember that first night, Cool Night?" Mabel says.

"Yes, I remember it all."

"I knew on the car ride over to Shepherdstown that day that I was going to kiss you. I couldn't stop thinking about you after the baseball game and I didn't care how or where, but I knew I was going to kiss you. I had to."

"I'm glad you did." My body yearns for her. We're both silent on the phone. I listen for her breath and wonder if she's replaying our first night together like I am. The streetlamp. Her clothes draped over the gaudy mirror. My lips against her neck, her tongue between my thighs. The morning sun dancing in through the plastic blinds and along our naked bodies. Her head against my chest. The first T-shirt. The morning coffee.

"I can't wait to kiss you again, Em."

I've dreamt about it a million times. More maybe.

MARCH

Thursday, March 1

"O'Malley signs law permitting same-sex marriage," I tell Mabel. "I'm reading it right now. It's scrolling across the news headlines."

"It's a start," Mabel says. I hear her sifting through schoolwork on the other end of the phone.

"Well, you don't sound too enthusiastic." I'm confused by her mellow tone. She's invested nearly three years, outside of law school, to volunteer and advocate for victories like this.

"It's a good start!" she says again with equal parts pep and sarcasm. "It's amended to not take effect until January first. The Maryland voters will ultimately decide."

"Wait. What?" I have trouble keeping up with even the most basic law lingo, despite being the child of a lawyer.

"It'll be on the ballot in November," she explains. "If it passes, the law will be enacted January first. If it doesn't, there will be moves to repeal it."

I click off the TV, annoyed by the outcome of what I thought was a pivotal moment.

"So, what do we need to do now?" I ask.

"From what I've gathered through meetings with the Love Rules Foundation, Roman Catholic authorities and African American religious leaders throughout the state have strongly opposed the legislation. We need at least a portion of their votes for this to pass. There are already many supporters within both of those groups, so at this point, it comes down to consistent, deliberate advocacy. Spread awareness. Let the people decide for themselves."

I interrupt. "I guess I'm just struggling to understand what the argument against it is?"

She continues without pause. She's spent years digesting what I'm just now trying to understand. "There's really two arguments against it. The first is that it threatens the best interest of society, which is just wrong on so many levels. Stable, healthy, commitments between two people have proven to improve social, mental, physical, and financial well-being. It's undeniable. Argument two is that it threatens religious liberties."

"What does that mean?"

"Like...Would a Catholic Church that didn't believe in same-sex marriages be required to marry two women? The answer is no. When O'Malley revised the bill, he made sure that religious liberties and freedoms were protected. There's a lot of mixed feelings on this one, but I personally am fine with the resolution. I just really don't care to get married somewhere that doesn't one hundred percent support my love, but I see the other side as well, I suppose. Kinda goes back to the separate but equal thing."

"Hmm." I'm letting all the gibberish soak in.

"Anyway, to soothe the worries of some hesitant lawmakers, the bill was amended to not take place until January, leaving time for a public referendum. So, what do we do? We go out there and we live our lives and we talk about LGBTQ rights when it's fitting, and hopefully those too religious to open their hearts to love will have a come-to-Jesus moment."

She pauses for a moment, likely remembering that I'm Jewish.

"Or…ya know…come to God moment. This is about giving every single adult the freedom to choose love. To be in love. To give love. To receive love. And to share in the protections that other committed loving couples already receive." She exhales deeply, the conversation exhausting her.

"All right, well, love is nice. I'm sure it'll all work out."

She chuckles at my abrupt conclusion to the conversation. "I think it will," she confirms.

"I miss you," I tell her. We've been obsessively talking. Making up for lost time, it seems. Texting through each morning, talking way too late into each evening. I haven't slept a full eight hours since the day she left me to head back to Durham.

"I miss you," she says, her voice warm and genuine.

"Why aren't you coming home for Easter?" I'd hop in the car and drive down to her right now if I felt comfortable leaving the brewery in someone else's hands.

"I can, maybe. I really want to, I just also really need to focus on the job hunt, and I have intentions of using the long weekend to avoid distractions and dive in."

"Wait, my dad has an opening. Right now. He has an opening. He was just talking about it to me."

"Really?"

"Yes! You should call him. They do all kinds of the make-you-feel-good law stuff. I think you might actually be interested."

She giggles at my ridiculous explanation of my dad's firm. "I remember him talking about his practice over dinner that one night."

"Yeah, I remember," I tell her. I remember every single thing about that summer.

She continues, "They assist with wrongful deportation, green cards, things of that nature?"

"Yep."

"Well, he's probably looking for a lawyer, though, and I won't be taking the bar for a while. Ideally, I can hop on as a paralegal somewhere. Get my foot in the door and make a little money while I study."

"I don't know what a paralegal is or what exactly he's looking for, but I'll text you his number and give him a heads-up that you'll be calling. If you're not a good fit for his firm, I'm sure he'll be happy to share some recommendations."

"Thank you." She pauses for a moment before asking, "What if your dad hires me and we end up giving this, as in you and I, a serious go when I get home, and nothing comes of it?"

"Something has already come of us. If it doesn't last, then maybe it just isn't meant to be. My dad will interview you based on my recommendation. He won't hire you because of it. He cares too much. He'll hire you if you're the right fit, and if you're the right fit for him and not me, then I'd consider our drawn-out rendezvous a win either way."

APRIL

Thursday, April 5

"I'm so excited to see you tomorrow!" I imagine this is what Christmas Eve feels like to young children. We've made plans for her to come over to my apartment for breakfast, and the anticipation is causing heart palpitations.

"I can't wait either. I'm just so happy with how the timing of everything worked out. I guess I have you to thank for that."

Mabel's initial call with my dad was followed up with a formal phone interview, which led to her upcoming Easter Monday interview. Since we don't do the Easter thing, it was easy for Dad and one of his Jewish coworkers to accommodate Mabel on her short visit. She interviews at nine o'clock at his office in Old Town Alexandria, and she will head back to school afterward.

I get to see her. Her family gets to spend Easter with her, and she gets to interview for her very first post-law school job. A win for all.

"Are you far?"

"Another two hours," she says. "You still at the brewery?"

I check my watch; 8:30. "I'm closing tonight, so I got another hour before I'm outta here."

"All right, well I'll let you know when I get to my parents."

"Drive safe."

* * *

At home, I cut up peppers, mushrooms, tomatoes, spinach, and shred loads of mozzarella in preparation for the veggie quiche I plan to make for Mabel in the morning. I hop in the shower and imagine slipping my fingers down Mabel's body like the water washing over me. As I throw on my pajamas, I hear a knock on the door. It's 10:45 p.m.

A neighbor, maybe?

I toss the towel wrapped around my head over the bathroom door and shake my hair free before hustling to the front door to peek through the peephole.

There she is.

I hastily undo the dead bolt, then the handle lock and swing the door open.

"I couldn't wait until the morning," Mabel says, pushing her way into my apartment and flinging the door shut behind her. She grabs my face in her soft freckled hands and kisses me hard. Again, and again, and again.

Her lips warm and freeing against mine. Her tongue slides in and out and I feel every ounce of my being light up. Years of pent-up passion, unraveling against my front door.

I lead her back to my bedroom, our lips still attached as I lay her down and crawl on top of her.

"I missed you," I whisper, our hands interlocked. I don't want to rush through this moment. I've been imagining it for years. I reach up her shirt and slide it off. She does the same to me. I unclasp her bra and run my hand gently from her ear to her breast. Her body lifts and presses against mine. She pulls me down beside her, so that we're lying side by side, our eyes entranced with one another.

"I want all of you," she moans as she pulls off my shorts. I unbutton her jeans and slip them off. Together, bare skinned and bold, we spend the next two hours rediscovering each other with our hands and our mouths, tracing our bodies, careful not to let a spot of skin go untouched.

Friday, April 6

"Good morning," Mabel whispers as she brushes strands of my hair behind my ear.

The early sun rushes in through the shutters. I smile as I take in this fairy-tale moment. "Best morning," I tell her. Her face scrunches joyfully at the cheesiness of it all.

"Coffee?" I roll out of bed and toss her a shirt and a pair of shorts. I know she needs something as she's still naked and she didn't carry a bag in with her.

"Thank you and yes, please."

She slips on the clothes, follows me out of the bedroom and into the living area. "You've upgraded from the trailer."

"I loved that place."

My apartment looks eerily like Annie's spot in Asheville. It's not quite as elegant or messy, but it offers the same modern, adult vibe. Exposed brick, enormous windows, and an open floor plan. I hand Mabel a cup of steaming black coffee, open the shutters, and we cuddle into my gray tweed living room couch, her knee against mine.

"I see you still have the picture I painted you. It's sweet you've kept it all this time."

"It was the first thing I hung up," I tell her. I recall tacking it up just beside my bed, the same place it was in the trailer.

I watch her scan the space. The rust leather corner recliner, the healthy fig plant, the muted, black-framed, mountain pictures that hang on the wall behind us.

"Simple. Modern. I like what you've done here, and the smell. Apple pie?"

"It's the bakery downstairs. I know." I nod my head assuredly. "It's drool-worthy. Pretty sure I'm their best customer."

Eventually, I bake the quiche and we spend the morning nibbling, sipping, and touching. It's the easiest of Saturdays, and when my alarm interrupts at 11:15, I irrationally debate closing the brewery for the day so that I don't have to leave her.

"Time for work, huh?" She hops up from the couch and ends my debate for me. She heads back to the bedroom to gather her clothes from the floor. I follow her.

"Here, let me help you make your bed."

As we pull the sheets up, she says, "Maybe my brother and I will swing by the brewery. You guys close at nine or ten tonight?"

I've never met her brother, but rockets erupt at the thought of seeing her again so soon.

"It's ten on Friday and Saturday. That would be awesome if you guys came."

"After dinner. We'll be there."

She grabs my hand in hers and leans in for a soft kiss before heading toward the front door.

"I already miss you," she says in her half-moon smile before letting herself out.

* * *

Journal: Friday, April 6, 2012

She belongs here.

* * *

"Em." Mabel leans over the bar to grab my attention. I hurry over to her and her brother.

One look at her sweet smile and the bustle that accompanies a standard Saturday evening suddenly feels as simple as the lazy morning we shared together.

"Hi, guys!" I greet them, excitedly.

"Emma, this is my brother, AJ."

AJ is handsome. He wears the same dark freckles across his cheeks as Mabel. His wavy hair is a bit lighter and his eyes, dark brown. I'm guessing he's five-eleven, broad swimmer shoulders, though I think I remember Mabel saying he was into tennis. He holds out his strong hand to shake mine. "Great to meet you, Emma," he says in a similarly raspy tone, but in a much deeper octave.

I notice Mabel eyeing up her brother's reaction and when he smiles, she smiles too.

"Same," I tell him. "What are ya'll drinking tonight?"

AJ perks up. "Mabel was telling me about some beer you drank on your birthday? A key lime?"

"Yes, yes! Santa's on Vacation." I carefully pour two pints with a quarter inch of foamy flavor on top. "It's on me," I whisper.

I sneak away from time to time, when the rush allows, to chat with Mabel and AJ. From conversations with Mabel, I knew they had a nice relationship, but it's enjoyable to witness. Their chatter flows from the moment they sit down, and in my brief visits, they throw me into their banter.

As the night nears closing, I see both Mabel and AJ are on their final sips. I pop in to gather their empty glasses. "You guys need anything else?"

Ignoring my question, I see AJ spruce up his posture to prepare for his final argument of the night. "Emma, now what do you think of social media? I'm against it, Mabel is for it. It's polluting us, though. I mean, to stay relevant I've gotta do Facebook and Twitter and now there's this Snapchat and Instagram? It's outta control!"

I direct my attention toward Mabel to get her opinion on it. "Mabel, what are your thoughts?"

She also ignores my questions and looks toward her brother. "Emma is not a fair tiebreaker on this one, AJ. She doesn't use social media." She looks up at me. "Do you even know what it is?"

"I do know what it is, and I do use it! There's a Holy Local page. Are you both following?"

Mabel snaps with a pompous glare, "I am a hundred percent certain you don't manage that page."

"I don't, but I do look at it sometimes."

The three of us chuckle. They throw back their last gulp. "We're gonna head out, Em," Mabel says as she slips on her coat.

AJ stretches out his hand. "It was so great to meet you, Emma. The beers were awesome."

"Glad you enjoyed."

Mabel leans in and plants a quick warm kiss on my cheek. "Are you free in the morning?"

"I gotta be here at eleven forty-five again. Why don't you come over when you get up?"

Saturday, April 7

"You couldn't sleep either?"

"Not a bit," Mable confirms. "I felt like I was seventeen, sneaking out of my parents' house this morning." We giggle as she follows me back to my bedroom and we crawl under the covers.

It's 4:23 in the morning; I've never been so happy to wake before the sun.

She curls up into me and we kiss until we're undressed. I run my hand up her thigh and deep inside her, warm and wet. We touch until exhaustion, then we sleep until the first signs of light tiptoe into the bedroom.

In her first waking moment, she asks, "Any interest in joining my family for Easter?"

"I'd love to, but Uncle Joey is coming into town today. I have one of my employees closing up the bar tonight so I can spend some time with him and my dad in Alexandria. And tomorrow we have a full brew day lined up. Apparently, Uncle Joey has some killer new recipe, so we're gonna give that a go tomorrow."

"Ahh, okay. That sounds nice. Well, I'd like to see ya once more before I head back to Durham."

"Any chance you can swing by tomorrow night? After dinner? You can stay?"

"Why don't I swing by. I won't stay. I want to make sure I'm rested and ready to go on Monday morning, but I'll come spend a couple of hours with you."

"Perfect." I don't bother fighting her on staying over. I've learned in our short stint of obsessive conversation that when it comes to her important tasks, she gives it her full and undivided attention. I admire that kind of dedication. One of the reasons I think she'll do well under my dad's leadership.

Sunday, April 8

"Did you have a good Easter dinner?"

We're curled up on my couch, under a chunky cream throw blanket, drinking turmeric tea.

"I did. It was just AJ, my parents, and my grandmother. I almost overdid it on the cookies. I ate five, but AJ ate thirteen. So basically, I ate zero and he ate eight."

I shake my head in confusion. "That makes absolutely no sense."

"It does. How was your day with your uncle and dad?"

I'm still confused, but I brush it off with the hope that she enjoyed her five or zero cookies. "It was good," I share. "We're bringing back a blueberry saison that we brewed during my summer in Asheville, so I'm excited for that. But get this—we brewed a beer called Sweety, You're a Sour Lemon. It's Uncle Joey's recipe, and my dad titled it."

"What a name!" Mabel laughs.

"We'll see how it turns out, but it's packed with pineapples, lemons, and limes. We'll serve it with a dash of sea salt. I'm expecting a refreshing summer ale."

"Sounds good." She nods.

"But it gets better! We're gonna can it and sell it in four-packs. The can labels are going to feature a flamboyant gay man dressed in rainbow everything and the beer name will be in a bubble as if he is speaking, 'Sweety, You're a Sour Lemon.'"

Mabel is uncontrollably laughing now. I continue, "Listen. Listen! On the bottom of the can, it'll say 'Don't be a sour lemon, vote YES for love in November.'"

"Absolutely brilliant!" Mabel shouts excitedly.

"We're gonna release it in June for Pride Month, and we'll run it through election day on November sixth. One hundred percent of the profits will go to groups that are actively fighting for marriage equality specifically in the state of Maryland. Organizations like Maryland for Marriage Equality, Maryland Black Family Alliance, and Freedom to Marry."

Mabel is beaming. "That is phenomenal."

"I'm excited about it. Apparently, Uncle Joey and Dad had been brainstorming this idea for months."

"It's an awesome idea." Mabel smiles sweetly. "You're lucky to have such a great family."

"I am, I know." I haven't stopped talking, so I switch topics. "Speaking of my dad, how are you feeling about the interview tomorrow?"

"I was a little nervous, kind of, at first. But I'm not anymore. I'm sure I'll have some game-day jitters." She smiles, knowing I appreciate a good sporty reference. "But I've read through his website and I've done my research on the work they've tackled. It seems like a great fit for me. I'm lacking some of the qualifications they're looking for. The obvious one being professional experience, but at the same time, I'm less expensive. I'll work hard and, you know, if he's thinking long term, maybe I'm someone he can train and mold and have around for some time."

"You're gonna do great."

"Thanks, Em."

Mabel checks her watch. It's nearing 9:00 p.m. She puts her mug down on the glass coffee table and scoots up close to me. "I gotta leave in a minute, but I wanna tell you something."

I put my mug down too and offer her my attention.

She grabs both of my hands and looks me in the eyes.

"I love you, Emma June. I'm telling you now because I've been holding it in for nearly four years."

Abrupt. Concise. Unexpected. I can't recall a more holy or happy moment.

"I love you, Mabel Ann."

"Good." She smiles wide. "That's good. I'm gonna go now."

We stand and wrap our arms around each other, squeezing out enough love to get us through the next month until she's home again.

Until she's home for good.

Monday, April 9

I roll over to a clock that reads 8:02. I stretch my body out and realize I haven't felt so rested in months. Mabel texted when she got home, but instead of talking to me late into the evening as we had grown accustomed to doing, she headed to sleep to ensure she was well rested for her interview.

I text Mabel an encouraging message just before her interview and I twiddle my thumbs over coffee and news until she calls around ten.

"I'm on the squad!"

"You were offered the job?"

"I was."

She proceeds to tell me how she met with my dad and another one of his employees. The job will include some entry-level research, paperwork, and even receptionist duties, but they've offered to pay for her to take the bar exam and then readjust her role and pay upon the completion of it. "Turns out that I was right in line with what they were looking for," she says. I can see her bright eyes and big grin through the phone. "I gotta call my parents!" she exclaims. "They're gonna be pumped that I'll be moving back in for a bit."

Moments later, my dad calls.

"I'm assuming you heard the good news?"

"I did. She's the one, huh?"

"She's perfect."

She really is.

Other than giving my dad a heads-up that Mabel was going to make an initial call, the two of us have not mentioned her in our conversations. His work is his passion. He's invested valuable years into its success, and I knew he would only hire her if she was the ideal candidate for the position. There was no reason to discuss it until a decision was made.

"She's passionate, well-spoken, and appears to be very driven. I'm excited to have her on the team."

"I'm excited for you. I think she's pretty great too."

Journal: Wednesday, April 18, 2012

There was only a sliver of your smile in the sky tonight.
Pie makes me think of how sweet you are.
I am 298 miles, 2 states, and 336 hours away from kissing your cheeks.
What a wonderful feeling you are.

JUNE

Saturday, June 9

"Let's rage!"

I fling myself around to find Millie and Jane barging through the front door of the brewery. My jaw drops. "What are you guys doing here?"

"We told you we were road tripping. You didn't think we'd pop in?"

The three of us have an ongoing text message thread where I shared all about my magical reconnection with Mabel and how she got the job with my dad, which they claimed took U-Hauling to a whole new level. In the same thread, they had shared that Jane had six weeks off for summer and their precisely detailed road trip schedule around the country most definitely did not include a stop in Frederick, MD.

"You guys." I hurry from around the bar to hug them. "I can't believe you're here. I took off today, and Mabel's coming. And my dad will be here! You know we have a drag show brunch from ten to noon today, right?" I'm babbling in jubilation.

"We know it all, and we're here for the brunch. We spoke to Mabel. We got her number from Tobin, who had to ask Karen for it, but never mind the logistics. Surprise!"

"Come here, come here." I wave them toward the bar. "We've got a few minutes before the bulk of the crowd will roll in. Let me share some of my favorites with you."

I pour them tasters of the whole draft line and fill them in on our Pride fundraiser involving Sweety, You're a Sour Lemon. They find it hysterical, and they buy two four-packs to help carry them through the rest of their trip.

Dad, Mabel, Louie, and Max all trickle in right around 9:30. Mabel must have let them in on the surprise visit from Millie and Jane because the six of them hastily knock out introductions before my dad throws down his credit card, eager to buy the first round.

By 9:45 we're a pile of old friends huddled around a taproom table, dollar bills in hand, sharing embarrassing stories, awaiting the start of the show.

* * *

"It was so great to see you guys!" I say, hugging both Jane and Millie at the same time in a tight embrace. "You sure ya can't stay?"

"We've got a strict schedule, you know that."

I hand them both a free Holy Local pint glass, T-shirt, and a sticker. They thank me endlessly and praise the space and the beers while I walk them through the crowded brewery and let them outside into the heavy summer heat. "Until next time, my friends."

"Until next time!" They wave and off they go.

Mabel slaps the seat beside her upon my reentry. "Em, what do you think?" she asks. "Are the O's gonna beat the Phillies today to win the series?"

"Yes," I say confidently. "I'm sure of it. Put the money on the Orioles."

My dad has had ongoing gambling action with the neighborhood bookie since as far back as I can recall. I know that's why this conversation started.

"I'm placing it!" Dad exclaims.

"And listen," Mabel chimes in, confidently. "I know it's early, but I bet they sweep the Pirates next series as well."

"Bold! But what the hell. I'll bet the lock on the sweep as well." Dad winks at Mabel. "Drinks on me if that one plays out."

I roll my eyes. His bets are usually twenty dollars at most, yet he acts as if he's a part of some big illegal gambling ring. "Gosh, you've got quite the confidence in your rookie employee, eh, Dad?"

"She's no rookie, Em." Dad high-fives Mabel.

"I'm the favorite employee, Emma, duh." The table laughs at her boozy remark.

"She is," Dad confirms. "The team is aware, and everyone is handling it quite well."

Dad's work team is like family, and it warms my heart knowing that Mabel has been well received, especially by him.

* * *

Mabel and I stumble back to my apartment around five and call in wings from the restaurant across the street. Officially, she lives at her parents, but she stays over most nights. I don't ever want her to leave, and it doesn't hurt that my apartment shortens her hour commute into Alexandria by ten minutes.

"I hope the referendum passes in November," she says, stumbling on to the couch.

Such a random topic to bring up after a day of baseball discussions and beer drinking. "Me too. What made you think of that?"

"Because I wanna get married one day."

"To me?" I ask.

"Maybe." She looks over with a kiss-me smile, so I hurry over and hop on the couch next to her.

"You do want to marry me!"

"Maybe," she says again in laughter. I kiss her neck and snuggle in beside her.

"I read this study," she says, "that people who oppose same-sex marriage generally think that those in same-sex relationships are more promiscuous and are more likely to have casual sex and be unfaithful."

"Well, that sounds like every twenty-five-year-old?" I joke, kind of.

She shoves me playfully and carries on. "In my unimportant opinion, every adult is entitled to do with their bodies and minds as they wish, but these thoughts are ridiculous. They're based on ignorance."

"For the record," I interrupt. "Your opinions are valid, and well thought out, and courteous, and they do matter."

"To you, maybe."

"Well, don't get greedy. Aren't I enough?"

She chuckles and continues, "People are just so close-minded, so stuck in their beliefs. There are promiscuous gay people and promiscuous straight people and there are very happy, content, faithful beings of all sexualities. I just can't believe this is even still a discussion. It seems insane that we're leaving our future together up to other humans, up to our neighbors."

"So you're saying we have a future together?"

She lets out another giggle followed by a deep sobering breath. "I'd like that."

We sit in silence, letting the very real concerns of her rant wash over before I assure her, "Our neighbors will come through for us."

And I pray they do, because I would like, very, very much, to marry Mabel Ann one day.

JULY

Sunday, July 1

"I can't believe this is the first time I've been to your house." Mabel is driving us up the long gravel road that leads to the modest brick rancher she grew up in. She picked me up from the brewery around five to join her for her dad's fifty-third birthday dinner.

"You've been missing out." Mabel grins. "It's a good place to be."

Her childhood home sits amidst twenty-five acres of rolling hills. Her family once housed a half a dozen pigs, two horses, and a small herd of black angus cattle, but they've slowly sold off the animals in the years following Mr. Pickett's stroke. Since then, Mrs. Pickett sectioned off a few acres for corn, a few for lavender, and she still tends to the large wire coop that holds thirty or so plump chickens. The rest of the land gets chewed up and spun into hay twice a year.

According to Mabel, the farm was always more of a hobby than an income. Mr. Pickett plays the stock market for a living. I don't understand it well, but it seems to suit him. He was able to buy this farm and send AJ and Mabel to their undergraduate studies free of loans. Mrs. Pickett runs the art gallery downtown, which also started as a passion project but has evolved into a low-maintenance city staple that Mable claims "covers the groceries and gas."

I carry in a dozen sunflowers, and both Mabel and I are greeted with a warm hug from Mrs. Pickett as we step into the kitchen.

Their house is charming. White kitchen cabinets. Decorative wood-framed windows. Aged thin-planked floors scuffed from splattered cooking oil and years of bare feet. A red teapot whistles as Mrs. Pickett shuffles us into the family room. "Emma, honey, come in, come in!"

I met Mabel's parents for the first time in May, just after Mabel's law school graduation. She brought them into the brewery, and we made small talk for an hour over a couple of beers. I comped the bill, but her dad slipped a hundred dollars into the tip jar for the staff, a gesture I found to be most notable. I must have also left a decent first impression because since our first visit, they frequently pop in for a beer, most often without Mabel.

"What's up, Emma?" AJ hops up from the floor for a hug. Mr. Pickett is in his recliner. His left arm, as expected, hasn't shown any improvement, and though he's made major strides with his left leg, his mobility isn't what I imagine it once was. I hustle over to him and lean in for a hug before he can consider pulling himself out of the chair. "Happy Birthday, Mr. Pickett."

"I wish you'd start calling me Scott." He smiles weakly. "Thanks, sweetie."

I snoop around the main floor, stumbling into the sunroom in the back of the house where I find a large canvas leaned up against a tall black easel. It's similar in style to the painting Mabel gifted me four summers ago. It must be her work. Pencil and watercolor. Two women, their backs against each other. The visible arm of each lies stretched out behind them, their fingertips just barely touching. One has sunflowers laced like music notes into strands of her midnight hair. The other is dressed in purple lilacs. The sun is setting in peaches and blues, the ocean is calm, the beach is empty.

It's Mabel and me. It's Chincoteague.

"It's us, if you're wondering." I feel Mabel walk up beside me just as I've pieced it all together.

"When did you have time to paint this?" I question without taking my eyes off the intimate masterpiece.

"When I'm not at work and not with you."

"That's like a total of four minutes since you've been home," I tell her as I admire the details, the beauty, the memory.

She ignores my comment. "Every day of that summer felt like vacation, ya know? Even this night, that didn't end exactly as I would have wanted it to."

I smile at her. "It was a good summer."

"It still does, ya know." She grins as she kisses my cheek. "Still feels just like vacation with you." She lovingly bumps her hip against mine before heading back into the kitchen to assist her mom with dinner.

NOVEMBER

Saturday, November 7

"This is the very first Saturday that I haven't spent working or drinking at the brewery."

It's been nearly a year since I opened Holy Local Brewery. Our operation, thanks to my incredible staff and the long-distance support from Uncle Joey, is stable and reliable and I don't have a bit of fear leaving the crew to handle the show on their own.

"I'm honored." Mabel grins. "I sure hope this is worth it."

We drive an hour and a half west of Frederick to the quiet mountain town of Cumberland, Maryland and park in the train station lot. Mabel grabs us each a cappuccino from a street vendor and by eleven a.m. we're boarding a diesel locomotive for an afternoon fall foliage tour through the Alleghany Mountains.

I peer around at our leaf-peeping neighbors as we shuffle toward our seat. There are men and women of all ages aboard, eager to see the spectacle of autumn, some dressed in knit sweaters, some in Bean boots, others draped in flannel blanket scarves.

"If your apple-pie apartment were human, it would be these people, on this train," Mabel whispers as we settle into our little cubbyhole booth.

We're sitting across from each other, a small table between us.

Within minutes of sitting, the train blares its keen horn and we chug forward. We travel the windy trail across rusted bridges, through steamy historic tunnels, and over broad photo-worthy landscapes. Everything is dressed in striking coppers and golds and crisp apple reds.

"It's pretty magical, huh?" Mae smiles, not taking her eyes off the deep valleys, speckled with charming farm homes.

The two of us, together, it is magical. I reach for her hand and squeeze it tight, wondering if her heart, like mine, still bursts into fireworks when we touch.

She wraps her other hand around mine, tearing her eyes from the window to face me. "I can't believe I let all these years go by without ya, Em." Yesterday's landmark victory for equal marriage rights in Maryland has us both feeling overly grateful. "Four and a half years ago you walked into Pickle's Pub. Can you believe it's been that long since we met?" I feel my face redden at the memory.

"I remember," Mabel says, "going home that night and not being able to sleep because I could only think of you. Your voice, our conversation. How beautiful you were. You are." She smiles softly. "I never stopped thinking about you. There were other women, sure. We were miles away from each other and we went months on months without speaking a single word, but you were always, always on my mind. I thought that maybe I'd find my way back to you one day and you would magically be single and open to talking, to dating even." Her soft smile stretches into an elated chuckle, apparently thrilled that her old thoughts have become reality. "I'm just so happy that we're together."

The years apart scroll through my memory. The miles, the mountains, the river, the whiskey, the women, the art, the beers, the truck, the chances, the states, the timing, the love. It all led to this. To her and I. To us.

"I'm happy too," I share with a squeeze of her hands.

"I've got something for you." Mabel lets go of my hands, reaches into her coat pocket, and pulls out a small chestnut leather box. My heart picks up speed. She opens it, revealing a rose gold band with a circular diamond. My skin fires up. Simple. Brilliant. I can feel the pressure behind my eyes. Tears bubbling up.

"I wanna marry you, Emma June."

I inhale deeply, settling into the moment. The crisp November sun stretches in through the train window and wraps its glorious arms around her. Her seaweed eyes. Her maple hair. Her freckles. Her half-moon smile. The best summer. The rest of my life.

"I wanna marry you, Mabel Ann."

Bella Books, Inc.

Women. Books. Even Better Together.

P.O. Box 10543
Tallahassee, FL 32302

Phone: 800-729-4992
www.bellabooks.com